Miss Stanton Meets Her Match

A STANTON LEGACY NOVELLA

M.M. Wakeford

Copyright © 2024 M.M. Wakeford. All rights reserved.

The characters and events portrayed in this book are fictitious. Any similarity to real persons, living or dead, is coincidental and not intended by the author.

No part of this book may be reproduced, or stored in a retrieval system, or transmitted in any form or by any means, electronic, mechanical, photocopying, recording, or otherwise, without express written permission of the publisher.

It is illegal to copy this book, post it to a website, or distribute it by any means without permission, except for the use of brief quotations in a book review.

First edition.
978-1-7395071-5-2

www.mw-author.com

Contents

The Stanton Legacy 5
Stanton Family Tree 6
Preface 7
Chapter 1 8
Chapter 2 14
Chapter 3 22
Chapter 4 26
Chapter 5 31
Chapter 6 36
Chapter 7 42
Chapter 8 46
Chapter 9 55
Chapter 10 63
Chapter 11 73
Chapter 12 76
Chapter 13 83
Chapter 14 88
Chapter 15 93
Chapter 16 96
Chapter 17 110
Chapter 18 114
Epilogue 118
Afterword 124
About the author 125

Also by this author 126

The Stanton Legacy

Interconnected steamy historical romances set in England and America from the 1830s to the 1860s following two generations of the powerful and wealthy Stanton family.

Book 1: The Viscount's Scandalous Affair
An illicit affair set in late regency London between two unlikely lovers whose emotional and bumpy journey into love ends in a happily ever after.

Book 2: The Vixen's Unlikely Marriage
A steamy romance set in Victorian England featuring a marriage of convenience between two unlikely characters, a beautiful vixen and a virtuous clergyman, who nevertheless find themselves falling in love.

Book 3: The Bluestocking's Secret Obsession
A slow-burn but steamy friends-to-lovers romance set in Victorian England and America in the Civil War.

Book 4: The Viscount's Forbidden Love
An MM romance set in Victorian England with plenty of heart, angst and steam—and it does have a happy ending.

Stanton Family Tree

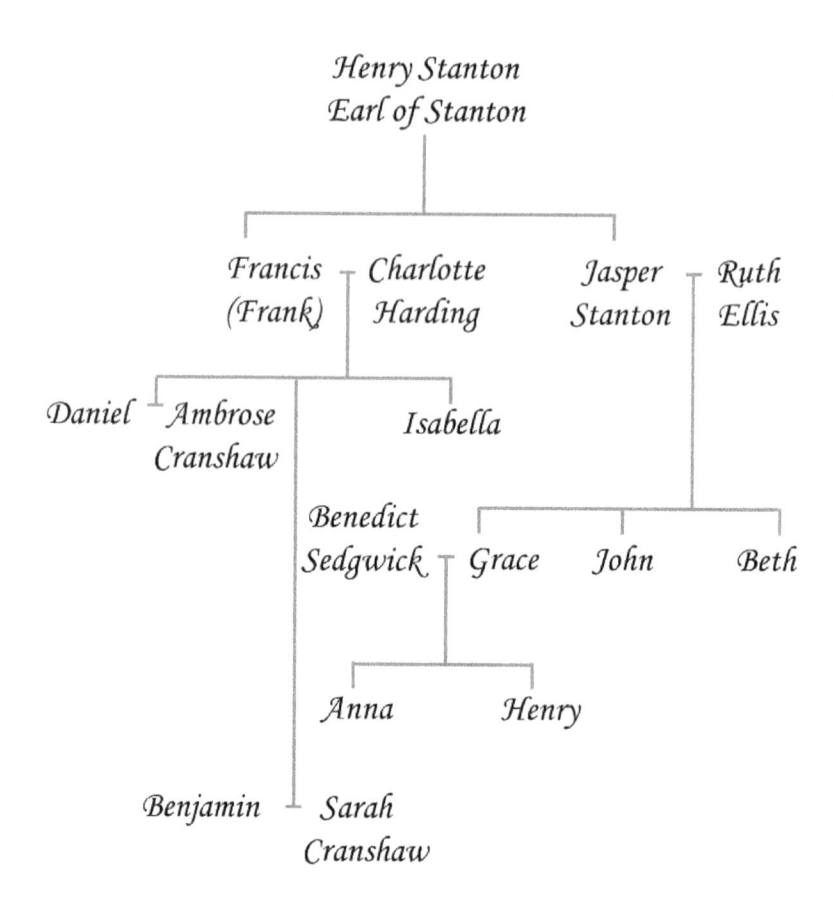

Henry Stanton
Earl of Stanton

Francis (Frank) — Charlotte Harding   Jasper Stanton — Ruth Ellis

Daniel — Ambrose Cranshaw   Isabella

Benedict Sedgwick — Grace   John   Beth

Anna   Henry

Benjamin — Sarah Cranshaw

Preface

This historical novella is a steamy age-gap, enemies-to-lovers romance with spin off characters from The Stanton Legacy. There are some very mild dominant/submissive vibes in the relationship between the two main characters, and despite the enemies-to-lovers trope, a bit of instalove to the romance too, as it does not take them long at all to fall for each other. There's also a few little homages to Jane Austen along the way and an echo of a scene from a popular TV drama, which some of you may spot and which I hope you'll appreciate.

You do not have to have read the other books in the series to enjoy this novella, as it can be read as a standalone, though your enjoyment of it will be enhanced if you are familiar with the rest of the timelines and characters.

Chapter 1

Isabella

August 1863

Isabella Stanton had determined from an early age that the fact of having been born female would not stand in the way of her doing what she desired. She was as capable in her intellectual abilities as either of her two older brothers, and thus she saw no reason why she should not take as active a role in managing her affairs as they did theirs.

Her opportunity to do so had come some two and a half years ago when she had inherited a substantial estate, Netherwick Hall, from her grandfather, the late Earl of Stanton. It had precipitated a difficult decision on her part—either to return with her family to their homestead in Ohio or stay behind in England to take charge of her newly inherited property. In the end, she had decided on the latter, much to her parents' chagrin. Such had been her determination to stand on her own two feet, as independently as it was possible, that her dearest papa had not had the heart to say no to her.

He had allowed her to stay on in England, though with the knowledge that she would be under the protection of her eldest brother, Daniel, who had inherited not just the title of Viscount Stanton, but the vast estate of Stanton Hall from their late grandfather. At Stanton Hall she would live, and from there she would see to her own estate, which lay some ten miles distant.

And so she had embarked on this novel life, at once a demure young lady of high rank, taking her rightful place in local society, and a lady of independent means, managing—quite successfully—her own, large estate. This was heady stuff indeed for a young woman of two-and-twenty years.

Of course, in these business endeavours, she did have the assistance of the Stanton estate manager, a gentleman by name of Ambrose Cranshaw. He it was that did the accounts and collected the rents, as well as oversaw any repairs to the buildings on her lands. However, he reported to her, and she was the one that took the most important decisions regarding her estate, such as the level at which rents were set for all her tenants, and who should have the tenancy of the main house, Netherwick Hall.

Over the last two and a half years, she had become quite proficient at her new role. She knew all her tenants well and visited her domain often. As for the main house, it had been let out for the past year to a local family of good standing, the Mortons, who were also distant relations of hers. They had moved to Netherwick Hall while major renovations were undertaken at their own estate of Stanbourne.

Now that these renovations were complete, the Mortons had moved back to their own home, and Netherwick Hall lay empty once more, in need of a new tenant. To this end, she was going there today to show the house to a Mr Wilson. She did not know much about the man except that he was a widower from Manchester with two young children, and that he had made his fortune in manufacturing.

In truth, she had grave reservations about letting out the grandness of Netherwick Hall to a man who had made his money in trade, and was therefore unlikely to be a gentleman by birth. It was not that she had anything against such a person, but she feared he might be uncouth in his manners—and thus unsuitable to take on the role of master of Netherwick Hall, even temporarily so.

As the carriage rattled along the road, she voiced these reservations to her companion on this journey, her estate manager, Ambrose Cranshaw. "How much do we know about this Mr Wilson, Ambrose?" she now asked. "What sort of a man is he? If he is not gentleman born, is he at least gentlemanly in his manner?"

To these questions, Ambrose merely smiled. "I cannot say for certain," he replied. "However, my correspondence with Mr Wilson these last few weeks has shown him to be a man of education, and the letter I received from his parish vicar vouched for his good character. I have also made enquiries as to his financial situation and have been reassured that Mr Wilson's income is more than comfortable. The rest, we shall have to find out upon meeting him."

"Yes, I suppose so," agreed Isabella.

Ambrose regarded her steadily. "Does it matter so very much that this Mr Wilson made his fortune in trade?"

Isabella flushed a little at the implied rebuke, the second she had received today, for her brother this very morning at breakfast had been at pains to remind her that their own father had made his fortune in America through the labour of his own two hands. She did not like to think of herself as a snob, for her mother, herself partly hailing from Spanish trade, had inculcated true Christian values in all her offspring. Yet Isabella could not explain why the notion of this Mr Wilson, a factory owner, taking possession of her beloved home, seemed so offensive to her.

Perhaps it was the notion that factory owners in the north of England had enriched themselves through the exploitative labour of their workers—when no such charge could be levied against her own father, who had toiled from morning till night to build their homestead in Ohio. In her mind's eye, she saw these factory owners on a par with the plantation owners in

America's south who enriched themselves on the labour of their slaves.

But the matter went deeper than that. The factory owners depended on cotton imported from those American slave plantations, and their influence was such as to have made the British government's position equivocal towards the Confederacy which was at this time engaged in a protracted civil war against the Union in America. And Isabella was no impartial bystander of that conflict. No indeed, her position was most partisan, especially since her own brother, Benjamin, was currently a soldier fighting for the Union.

Just this morning, she had received a letter from him, telling her of the latest engagement at the battle of Gettysburg. Her relief at hearing he was alive was tempered by sadness at the news that their childhood friend Jimmy, who had enlisted alongside Benjamin, had sadly been killed. Isabella's worry about her brother, as well as about the rest of her family's safety in this war, had been great these past two years. Little had she known, on saying goodbye to Ma, Pa and Benjamin when they had returned to America in January 1861, that she would not see them again for a long time and that they would become embroiled in this civil war.

Over time, the Confederacy had come to be an evil entity in her mind, and any party that stood in its full or even partial support was, in her eyes, just as evil. Thus had Isabella formed a poor opinion of the factory owners of the north of England who continued to engage in trade with the vile Confederacy, if only to obtain the much needed cotton for their mills. Somehow though, it was difficult to articulate such a feeling, and she found it easier therefore to pretend her objections to Mr Wilson were based on social class rather than on a perceived connection with the evil forces that were at this time engaged in a fight against her family in America.

Now, faced with Ambrose's question, she scrambled for a suitable response. In the end, she gave him a little of the truth. "No," she replied, "it does not matter so much that Mr Wilson has made his fortune from trade, only the nature of the trade he has engaged in." She looked down at her clasped hands. "You may have an inkling, Ambrose, of my sentiments towards the mill owners who continue to engage in trade with the Confederate south for their cotton."

Ambrose was quiet for a moment, then got to the heart of the matter. "Has there been any news of Benjamin?" he asked gently.

She nodded, saying, "A letter arrived this morning, telling us he fought in the latest engagement at Gettysburg, which resulted in a great many casualties, including that of our dear friend, Jimmy."

"I am so very sorry to hear of it," said Ambrose, "but also relieved that your brother is unharmed."

Isabella bit her lip and blinked, trying very hard not to succumb to the tears that wanted to slip down her cheeks. "Yes, me too," she murmured. "You may think it most unchristian of me, Ambrose, but my first thought upon reading Benjamin's letter was to rejoice that it was Jimmy and not him that had been killed."

It was no good trying. A tear escaped from each uncooperative eye. Isabella wiped them away crossly as Ambrose spoke softly, "It is only natural to think of your loved ones first. Do not be too harsh with yourself, Isabella."

She sniffed and nodded. "Ambrose," she asked, "how long do you think this war is likely to go on?"

"I do not know," he said on a long sigh. "However, from what I have read, it seems this latest engagement at Gettysburg has been successful in stopping the Confederacy's advance on

Washington, despite the heavy loss of life. It may, I hope, prove to be the turning point in this war."

"I do hope so too," replied Isabella.

"And as for Mr Wilson," Ambrose said, returning to their earlier subject of conversation, "it is best we focus solely on the salient matter. Is he likely to be a good tenant—and by that I mean, will he take good care of the property he occupies and ensure the rent is paid in a timely manner?" He looked across at Isabella with a keen gaze. "It matters not whether you form a liking for the man or not," he added, "for we are not interviewing him for the role of a family friend. We will show him around Netherwick Hall and use our instinct to gauge whether he seems to be a trustworthy enough tenant."

"Yes, Ambrose," concurred Isabella, though in her heart she knew that she would be unable to avoid judging Mr Wilson and finding him wanting.

Chapter 2

Silas

Mr Cranshaw was late. They were due to meet here, at the entrance to Netherwick Hall, at half past ten, and according to Silas's pocket watch, it was now a good seven minutes past that appointed time. He disliked having his time wasted, not to mention the fact that the sun was beating unpleasantly down on his carriage this hot August day.

The air was stifling, despite the opened carriage window, and after a moment's consideration, Silas decided to venture out into the morning sunshine. His hat afforded him some protection from the sun, and there was a hint of a breeze to cool him down. He would take a turn around the house and inspect the exterior of his new home, or more accurately, his potential new home. He had not yet decided whether he would take on the tenancy of Netherwick Hall.

His steps took him past the wide staircase flanked on either side by decorative sculptures. He walked on, taking in the tall, rectangular windows set into the sand-coloured stone local to the area. The house was built in the Palladian style favoured by architecture of the early eighteenth century. It was undoubtedly grand and distinguished, but such things were of no great consequence for Silas. What mattered most to him was to have a home in which Theodora and Samuel could be comfortable.

It was eight months since the children had lost their mama—his dear wife, Ada, having been taken from them by scarlet fever—and two months since Silas had taken the decision to sell his controlling interest in the manufacturing business he had built up some two decades ago. For more years than he cared to remember, the management of his factories and vast workforce had taken much of his time, leaving him little to spare for his wife and children. Slowly, however, it had become clear that he could no longer sustain such a lifestyle when he had two motherless children to care for.

Of course, they had a governess and a whole army of household staff to take care of their immediate needs. At first, Silas had thought they could continue life as it was, just without Ada. He was quickly disproved of that notion. Ada's absence had left them all rudderless, most of all the children. Silas mourned and missed his wife with a dull but persistent ache. Theirs had been a good marriage. Even though there had not been any great romantic passion between them, they had suited each other well. Theirs had been a quiet but enduring love.

For several months after her passing, he had found it difficult to sleep alone in the bed he had shared all those years with Ada. Only recently had he become accustomed to it, though he still caught himself occasionally reaching out at night for Ada's comforting presence only to encounter thin air. He had taken to placing several long pillows beside him on the bed, so that when his arm reached out, it at least had something to clutch on to.

Perhaps he ought to think about marrying again. That was what his sister, Esther, had advised him to do in her last letter. She even had a suitable candidate in mind for the position, a lady by the name of Violet Corbett, a solicitor's widow. In theory, a second marriage was a sound idea. It would provide him with the companionship he missed and his children with a mother to care for them. Nevertheless, something in Silas shrunk from the prospect. He did not like the thought of bringing some strange lady into his household. Of course, after a period of acquaintance, such a lady would no longer be a stranger to them, but still, he found the notion distasteful. Ada was not to be replaced so easily.

On one thing, however, he had agreed with his sister—that he should sell up and move to Oxfordshire, close to where Esther lived with her husband, a doctor, and her family. And so here he was today, inspecting a grand mansion set within vast parkland and contemplating the life of a country gentleman. He had money aplenty to do it, yet he was not sure if the role would suit him. He was not idle by nature. Already though, he had thoughts as to what new ventures and investments he could enter into. The proximity of Netherwick Hall to Oxford, and to a train service to London, made it a good location to settle in. He would be near to Esther as well as be able to easily visit London for business whenever required.

He had by now reached the back of the house, which overlooked a set of ornamental gardens. In the distance, he could see the glimmer of water from a small lake. A frown knit his brow as he contemplated living in such surroundings. There would be far more space for the children to play outside, and the air would certainly be more sanitary than the smoky fog of Manchester. He turned his gaze back to the house which stood majestically before him, a three-storied rectangular building of grand proportions. The upkeep of such a place would be steep, he mused, though his pockets were deep enough.

He huffed derisively. What a turn up for the books to see him, Silas Wilson, an engineer's son, now living the life of a country gentleman. Of one thing he was certain though. He was not about to give himself airs and graces or wash away the humbleness of his past to pretend he was to the manor born. People would have to take him as he was—gruff, unpolished but canny when it came to making a profit. He would not ever apologise for who he was.

He continued on his perambulation around the house. Yes, he thought, this place would do nicely as a new home for himself, Samuel and Theodora. He had yet to see the interior, of course, and that might still sway the matter. If only this Mr Cranshaw would get here! It was a hot day, and he had no wish to dilly-dally. He stopped to take out a handkerchief and wipe the sweat that had gathered on his brow, then resumed his journey.

A short while later, he found himself once more at the front of the house, where a carriage was just this moment drawing up. From it alighted a gentleman, Mr Cranshaw no doubt, followed by a young lady of quality, if one were to judge the style and fabric of her dress. Silas frowned. Perhaps he had the wrong of it. Could this be a married couple also come to see the house with a view to renting it for themselves? Mr Cranshaw would surely not be so crass as to invite viewings from two parties at the same time.

As he stood observing them, the gentleman caught sight of him. With a smile, the man strode in his direction, the lady on his arm. "Mr Wilson, I presume," the man said in a softly-spoken voice.

Silas executed a short bow. "Yes, that is me, and you must be Mr Cranshaw."

The other man bowed his head in greeting. "Yes, indeed I am. And this here is Miss Stanton," he said, introducing his lady companion.

Silas bowed stiffly in her direction. "Miss Stanton," he said, in his naturally deep voice. He was not sure who this lady might be exactly, but he knew this estate belonged to the Stanton family. She must somehow be connected to it, although he did not know what a lady so young—for she could barely be a year or two above twenty—was doing in Mr Cranshaw's company on such a mission as this. Perhaps they were affianced and she was merely keeping him company? He shrugged internally, ready to dismiss her, when he observed the disdainful curl of her lips as she inclined her head in his direction.

"Mr Wilson," she said in a cool voice. "I do hope we have not kept you waiting very long."

Something in her tone made him bark out, "Long enough to have walked the perimeter of the house." He turned his attention to Mr Cranshaw and added, "And now I should wish to see the interior without further ado."

Mr Cranshaw smiled, unaffected by his brash manner. "Of course," he said. "Do let us get out of this dreadful heat at once." He rummaged inside a leather satchel he carried across the shoulder and took out a set of keys. "Do follow me, Mr Wilson."

With this, Mr Cranshaw walked up the front steps and inserted a key into the lock on the large wooden door, opening it to let them inside. Silas had enough courtesy to allow Miss Stanton to precede him into the large entrance hall. It was several degrees cooler there, a welcome respite from the humid heat outside. Bright light streamed through the tall windows and reflected off the chequered white and black tiled floor.

Silas studied his surroundings with a keen eye. It was illustrious and grand, as was to be expected, but along with the elegance was a bright and cheery aspect which he found curiously appealing. His attention was brought back to Miss Stanton as she addressed him haughtily. "If you have no objection, Mr Wilson, I suggest we begin the tour on the upper floors and then work our way down."

He nodded briskly. "Let us do so," he said, wondering at the young lady's surprisingly imperious manner, acting as if she owned the place. Surely it should be Mr Cranshaw doing the honours and showing him around the house, not this young chit of a girl. But Silas had no time for such musings. The important thing was that he see the house. If she wished to lead the way, then so be it. In silence, he followed Miss Stanton up the stairs, with Mr Cranshaw in the rear. She led him along a corridor then opened a door, saying as she did so, "This is the main bedchamber. It connects to a secondary bedchamber which is for the mistress of the house."

Ah yes, thought Silas sardonically, another quirk of the aristocracy—separate bedchambers for the master and his lady. God save him from the stupidity of the upper classes. He contented himself with a slight pursing of his lips and followed the young lady into the room, looking about him with interest. It was of a good size, the large windows giving it an airy feel. On one wall was a four-poster bed with a tall canopy in a rich blue fabric.

"It is said King George II once slept in this room as a guest of my ancestor, Lord Netherwick," Miss Stanton informed him in a self-important tone.

Silas ignored her speech and marched forward to the connecting door, opening it to enter the second bedchamber. Looking around him, he decided he would have no need of it as it was, but perhaps he could convert the room to a study or a private parlour. Satisfied, he opened the outer door and stepped into the corridor once more, casting an impatient glance back at Miss Stanton and Mr Cranshaw.

That gentleman behoved himself to say, with a point of his hand towards the corridor, "There are five further bedchambers and a bathing room along here. Please feel free, Mr Wilson, to take a look."

Silas nodded and did just that, walking purposefully from room to room and looking his fill. Once he was done, he returned to the main staircase and walked back down, pausing at the bottom to wait for his two companions. They came down at a more sedate pace and joined him in the entrance hall. Miss Stanton wore upon her face a look of frigid disapproval but did not deign address any further speech in his direction. All the better. He had no need for tedious prattle about much vaunted visitors to the house. Mr Cranshaw now took over, leading him through the rooms on the ground floor and blessedly saying little beyond the most necessary in the way of speech. By the time they had retraced their steps back to the entrance hall, Silas was decided on the matter.

As was his wont, he dove straight to business. "Mr Cranshaw," he said abruptly. "This house will do for me and my family. I should like to take possession of it in mid-September, if you please. Kindly draw up the necessary paperwork and send it to me."

He took a step towards the front door in preparation to leave but was halted by Miss Stanton calling out, "Mr Wilson, I am afraid the matter has not yet been settled. We have had interest from other parties with regards to Netherwick Hall, and it is too soon for me to have made a decision as to whom I shall rent the property to."

Silas swivelled around to face the young lady, treating her to one of his fierce stares—the one that almost always had his interlocutors quaking in their boots. Although Miss Stanton trembled, and a flush was visible on her cheeks, she stood her ground resolutely. Silas continued to peruse her with a steely gaze. Three facts were making themselves evident to him. Firstly, that Miss Stanton had told an untruth when she claimed there were other parties interested in renting Netherwick Hall. Silas had an instinctive knack for divining such things, and he was sure as sure could be that Miss Stanton had just told a fib.

Secondly, it seemed that Miss Stanton was the actual proprietor of this house and that she took an active role in managing her affairs—at least to the point of being the one to decide whom to rent the house to.

And thirdly, when angry and agitated, Miss Stanton's dark eyes burned with a passionate fire that was peculiarly seductive. In point of fact, Silas could not look away from the fieriness of Miss Stanton's gaze. He stared for a long moment before coming back to his senses and growling, "Miss Stanton, whatever the case may be with regards to other parties, they are not here right now but I am, and I am also willing to meet the terms set out by Mr Cranshaw in his correspondence with me. I do not see, therefore, that there is any need to postpone a decision on this matter." Addressing Mr Cranshaw, Silas continued, "I shall expect the contract papers within the week. Good day, Mr Cranshaw, Miss Stanton." And with that, he took his leave.

Chapter 3

Isabella

Isabella felt as if she would combust with the force of her anger. How dare that man address her the way he did? How dare he think the matter was settled when she had not yet pronounced her decision? Well, she would show him. Instead of contract papers being sent to Mr Wilson, he would be getting a cool letter of rejection.

"Whatever is brewing inside that head of yours, put it to one side until you have had a chance to cool your anger," said Ambrose at her side.

"That man was impossible!" huffed Isabella.

"He was certainly a little gruff in his manners," conceded Ambrose.

"So you can see, Ambrose, how impossible it would be to rent Netherwick Hall to such an individual," continued Isabella.

"I see no such thing," he replied. It was a good thing he was her friend as well as her estate manager, or else she would not have tolerated such insubordinate talk. With a scowl on her face, she let him escort her out the door and into the waiting carriage. Only once they were at last on their way back home did he explain himself. "Remember what I said earlier, Isabella, about it not mattering if you like the man or not. What we are looking to see is if he will make a good tenant, and on that front, I am reassured that he will."

Isabella gazed crossly at him. "And how have you reached this conclusion?" she asked sullenly.

"Well, let's see," replied Ambrose. "First of all, the fact he was punctual in arriving for this appointment, as opposed to us—" Here, Ambrose looked pointedly at her. Yes, it was true that they had been late setting out this morning, but that was only because of Benjamin's letter and the fact she had had to go back to her room to wash the tears she had shed from her face. Ambrose continued, "—added to the promptness in which he sent me the documents I requested, indicates to me that he will be punctual in all his dealings with us and in the payment of the rent."

Seeing that she was yet to be convinced, he went on, "Then there is the fact that the man has a straight-talking manner with no beating about the bush. It may not have made for the best in social graces, but I would much rather have that than deal with a glib and dishonest person who lays on a profusion of charm. I believe I know where I stand with Mr Wilson, and that is something that I can appreciate."

Isabella sniffed and bit out her response, "I take your point, Ambrose, but is it too much to ask for a modicum of good manners?"

At this, Ambrose smiled. "No, of course not. However, I hazard to hope that Mr Wilson is not entirely deficient in manners. I suspect his irascibility today was down to two things." At her raised brow, he elucidated. "First, having been kept waiting in this dreadful heat cannot have done much for anyone's temper, and second, he could not fail to have noticed the evident disdain with which you spoke to him. I suspect the man's pride had him speak a little more sharply than he might perhaps have done otherwise."

"So you are putting his rudeness at my door," snapped Isabella.

Ambrose gazed mildly at her, not responding. Eventually, her sense of fairness had her admit, "I suppose I was rather less than gracious. But there was something about him, Ambrose, that raised my hackles. I cannot put my finger on it."

"Were you not already predisposed to disliking him?" Ambrose enquired gently.

Isabella tapped her feet nervously, still agitated from her encounter with Mr Wilson. "Even so, there was something about him which I found... tremendously discomfiting." That look he had given her at the end, just before he delivered those parting words. It had been scorching. She had felt her cheeks flame and her heart pound madly in her chest. Her hands had trembled until she had clenched them into fists. Even now, several minutes later, her heart had yet to return to its normal beat.

She pictured Mr Wilson in her mind. He was of average height, but broad, almost burly in appearance. His well-cut jacket had done little to hide the strong, muscular frame beneath. He was not a handsome man, but his face was one that could not easily be forgotten. Isabella vividly recalled the brilliant dark eyes set under thick, straight brows that had skewered her with their stare, not missing a single detail.

Everything about Mr Wilson had exuded vitality and something else... some primal energy that had at once fascinated and scared her. As she had stood before him with fists clenched, she had caught in the warm air around them a hint of his strongly masculine scent, all of which had magnified the powerful presence of the man. She took a deep breath now and tried to put this disturbing memory from her mind. After a while, she looked across at Ambrose and asked, "So, you think we should offer him the tenancy of Netherwick Hall?"

Ambrose met her gaze. "I would be inclined to do so," he said softly. "However, the decision is entirely yours to make, Isabella."

She huffed. Well she knew that she would follow Ambrose's advice, as she did in most things. And he knew it too, confound him. A few moments more and she said, "Very well. Go ahead and send him the tenancy contract." In an undertone, she added, "I shan't have to see him at all, even if he is my tenant."

In this assessment, she was to be proved entirely wrong.

Chapter 4

Isabella

One month later

"Good day, Mrs Shaw," said Isabella, bidding farewell to one of the tenants on her estate. The Shaw farm was a small holding, only about fifty acres. It had been held by Mr Shaw's family for three generations until the farmer's untimely death two weeks ago, leaving behind a widow and five children, the oldest of which was a sixteen-year old youth, Peter.

It had not taken long for the vultures to come for their pickings. A neighbouring farmer, Mr Flint, had paid Isabella a visit yesterday to petition for the takeover of the Shaw farm. "The Shaws may stay on in the farmhouse," he had said magnanimously, "but you must see, Miss Stanton, that a young boy of sixteen cannot be put in charge of the farm itself. It is a difficult enough business to manage for a grown man, let alone a callow youth. I feel it is my duty, therefore, to take on that acreage and ensure it is properly managed. I would be much obliged, Miss Stanton, if you could arrange for the tenancy of the Shaw farm—minus the house itself—to be transferred into my name."

Isabella had regarded him coolly and replied, "I thank you, Mr Flint, for your concern about the management of the Shaw farm. It shows a great neighbourly spirit. However, I cannot at this time give you a response until I have investigated the matter more fully."

"There is little to investigate," had exclaimed Mr Flint stubbornly. "The Shaw farm has been left without anyone to tend to it. With the harvest upon us, it is most pressing to have the matter resolved swiftly. The quickest solution, as I see it, Miss Stanton, is for myself to do the right and honest thing and take on those additional acres, even though it will put far more work onto my shoulders."

"I would not want to burden you with such work, Mr Flint," Isabella had replied frostily, "if there could be any other way to resolve the situation. I promise to look into the matter as speedily as possible. Good day now." And she had dismissed the farmer who reluctantly had taken his leave.

First thing this morning, she had ridden out to the Shaw farm and had a talk with Mrs Shaw and her eldest son, Peter. Both had assured her that they were up to the task of taking on the running of the farm, and begged her not to let "Greedy Old Flint" take what was theirs. Isabella had been reminded of her own situation, and how she had been determined, upon inheriting Netherwick Hall, to manage her own affairs despite being a mere female. She saw an equal resolve in Mrs Shaw's eyes and perhaps that was why she had acquiesced to their request, on the condition that they could prove to her within three months that they were up to the task of running the farm. They had agreed to this with alacrity.

Now, Isabella made her way back to her horse. With easy grace, she perched onto the saddle and began her journey back home. She had barely travelled a few minutes before she heard a sharp cry coming from the stream on her right. She reined in her horse and listened. There it was again. It sounded like the cry of a child. Without hesitation, Isabella jumped down from her saddle and quickly tethered her horse to the trunk of a nearby tree. Then she hurried in the direction from which she had heard the cry.

Standing by the tall grasses along the bank of the stream, she saw two children—a girl of eight or nine and a boy a few years younger. In the same instant, she saw what had caused the cry. A small, roughly crafted wooden boat, presumably belonging to the boy, had floated out of his reach into the middle of the stream. As she strode in their direction, the boy leaned forward, making paddling motions with his hand to try to retrieve his boat. With dismay, she saw him lean a little further, but her cry of warning was too late. The boy fell into the water with a loud plop, followed by panicked screams both from himself and the girl.

Isabella reached the bank and held out her hand to the boy, but he had already drifted out of reach. She saw him flail and knew that something had to be done quickly. In a matter of seconds, she had pulled off her shoes. Then she was wading into the icy water, swimming with strong, measured strokes towards the boy. She grasped at his jacket and pulled him to her, treading water as the boy wrapped his arms tightly around her neck. Fortunately, the current was not too strong, but the water was icy, and they needed to get out of there quick if they were not to catch their death of cold.

With this unwieldy burden, she began to swim back to the shore, but the boy's attention was now back on his boat. "There it is!" he cried. "Oh, do please let us catch it." On an inward sigh, Isabella turned with the boy clutched in her arms and spotted the errant craft. She swam towards it and swooped it with one hand.

"Here, hold on to it," she instructed, needing that hand free to paddle back to the shore. The boy took it, holding it to his chest with one hand and clasping Isabella's neck most uncomfortably with the other. Taking a deep breath, she began the arduous task of swimming back to the shore. It was harder than she had anticipated, with the combined weight of the boy and her dress weighing her down. It took every effort she had to reach the banks of the stream, where the young girl stood, watching them anxiously. Isabella found one last reserve of strength to lift the boy into the girl's waiting arms, then to heft herself out the water.

She collapsed on the grass, panting breathlessly. She knew they could not linger like this, in their cold, wet clothes, but she needed a moment to gather her strength. She tried to think through what to do next. "Where is your home?" she puffed, still winded from her ordeal.

The girl was the one to answer. "It's the big house over that way," she said, pointing in the direction of Netherwick Hall, just under a mile away.

Immediately came the realisation who these children were. The Wilsons. Next moment came confirmation of this. "I am Theodora Wilson," said the girl, "and this is my brother, Samuel."

Her wits beginning to return, Isabella asked as she got to her feet and put her shoes back on, "How did you come to be alone so far from home?"

The children exchanged guilty looks. "Never mind," huffed Isabella. "We need to get to the house and quick. Come with me." Holding the sodden skirt of her dress in one hand, she led them to her horse, which stood passively munching on some grass. "We shall have to ride together," she decided. That would be the quickest way back to the house. She looked at Theodora. "If I help you up onto the saddle, can you hold Samuel in your arms?"

The girl nodded wordlessly. Swiftly, Isabella assisted Theodora up onto the saddle, then lifted Samuel up high in her arms and handed him over to his sister. "Hold him tight, now," she urged. Next, Isabella untethered the horse, and with the rein in one hand, climbed onto the saddle behind the children. It was a tight and awkward fit, especially having to sit side saddle with the heavy weight of her wet skirt, but they would have to bear it for the short journey to the house. With a light nudge of her foot, she set them moving at a brisk canter in the direction of Netherwick Hall.

Chapter 5

Silas

"Where on earth are they?" Silas boomed at Miss Grainger with what was no doubt a fierce expression on his face, judging by the governess's nervous reaction. But he did not care much at this point if he was being intimidating. All he wanted to know was the whereabouts of his missing children.

"I—I do not know," she stammered. "I only left them for a minute to go upstairs and fetch Samuel's coat, for it has turned a little chilly. When I came back, they were gone!"

"Have you searched the gardens, gone down to the lake?" he barked.

"Yes, sir," fluttered Miss Grainger. "We have searched everywhere."

"Obviously not, since you have not found them." He turned to one of the footmen hovering by the door. "Search every nook and cranny of the house for them," he ordered. If they were in the house somewhere, they would soon be found. If they were not, then no doubt they had gone wandering about, despite being told many times not to do so. In which direction would they have gone?

Silas stood still, looking in the distance. This morning at breakfast, Samuel had brought down the wooden craft he had made with Theodora's help and proudly shown it off. There had been talk of wanting to test it in the water and a promise that they would do so later in the afternoon. Could it be the children had gotten impatient and decided to take their boat to the lake? But no, Miss Grainger had said that area had been searched. *Think, Silas, think.*

Perhaps they had decided to try out their boat in the stream that ran to the east of Netherwick Hall. Its course began some three quarters of a mile from the house. Silas pursed his lips angrily. Just wait until he got hold of those errant children of his. If he rode his horse, he might catch them up before they reached the water.

In quick strides, he made his way towards the stable. "Saddle Phoenix for me and make it quick," he called out to the groom. In moments, he was on his horse and galloping towards the stream. He tried not to let worry overcome him, but he could not help a tight constriction in the region of his heart. Please God, he prayed. Let them be all right.

He was halfway to his destination when he saw a rider coming in his direction. Once he was a little closer, he spotted Samuel and Theodora mounted at the front, looking wet and bedraggled. The two horses drew to a halt beside each other, and that was when he identified the person sitting behind his two children. Miss Stanton. A very wet and shivering Miss Stanton.

There was no time to argue about what had happened. "Give Samuel to me," he barked, reaching for his son. Once the boy was secure in his arms, he gritted out, "The house. Now," and then set off in the direction of Netherwick Hall. No words were spoken as both horses rode furiously towards the house, not stopping until they reached the front steps. Silas jumped down to the ground and lifted Samuel off the horse. Then he turned to his daughter and helped her down too. "A hot bath and a change of clothes, then bring them down to the parlour," he instructed the servants that had run towards them.

Only then did he turn to Miss Stanton, who remained on her horse. "What are you doing still up there?" he asked irritably. "Come down."

She merely shook her head. "I shall return home now," she said, lips trembling with cold.

He felt a wave of red hot anger rush through him. "I said come down!" he roared. In two strides, he was at her side, gripping her waist to lift her off the horse, despite her loud protestations. He set her on her feet and took a good look at her. The pale blue gown she wore was plastered to her skin. He could not help but notice the rise and fall of her generous breasts, and their puckered tips that peeked beneath the surface. For half an instant, his gaze was transfixed on that glorious sight. Then all at once, common sense returned.

"You will catch your death of cold if you do not get out of these wet clothes right away," he grunted, his hands still around her waist. He felt her tremble in his hold and wondered briefly if it was due to the cold or to something else. He forced himself then to let go and step back. "Go up now to the pink damask room," he said gruffly. "I will have a hot bath sent up to you and something dry to wear. Join me in the main parlour once you are done." She opened her mouth as if to argue, but one look at his determined face must have convinced her otherwise. She simply nodded and hurried off into the house.

He took a moment to compose himself before barking out orders to have a hot bath sent up to Miss Stanton post-haste. Remembering she needed dry clothes, he summoned another servant to go fetch something suitable to wear from Miss Grainger, whom he judged to be around the same size as Miss Stanton. "And please ensure Miss Stanton's clothing is washed and pressed in time for me to escort her back to her home later this afternoon," he added.

"Yes, sir," said the maid, bobbing a curtsy before rushing to do his bidding.

Next, he strode over to the kitchen, causing his cook no small amount of surprise. He ignored her perturbation at having the master enter her domain. "Mrs Jones," he instructed crisply. "We shall need soup for our luncheon, something warm and hearty to help the children and Miss Stanton overcome their chill."

"Yes, sir," mumbled the cook.

"And seeing as we have an unexpected guest dining with us," he went on, "please see to it that the meal does us proud. I shall expect a good joint of meat, preferably beef, some delicately steamed fish with white sauce, and a pie of some sorts, as well as a good amount of vegetables to serve with them. And for sweets, I think a jam pudding and a lemon tart would do nicely."

Mrs Jones's mouth gaped and her eyes went round with shock, but she soon had herself in hand. "Yes, of course, sir," she said. He left the kitchen then, satisfied that the matter was in good hands. He paid his servants extremely well and expected excellent service in return. They had to this day never once let him down—no one, that is, except for that Miss Grainger, who had been derelict in her duties today. He would have words with her about it in the morning.

He walked to the parlour and sat down to wait for his children and Miss Stanton. To his children, he would have a stern lecture to give. To Miss Stanton, he would express his gratitude—for though he did not yet have the details of what had occurred, it was clear that she had rescued Samuel from some mishap in the water. Then, they would eat their luncheon, after which he would personally escort Miss Stanton back to her home. And that would be all. He certainly was not going to indulge in a lustful infatuation with a lady so many years his junior. One, moreover, who had shown nothing but disdain for his person. Hell and damnation! A man had his pride. He was not about to make himself a laughing stock over a chit of a girl. Of that, he was determined.

Chapter 6

Isabella

The hot bath went some way towards warding off the shivers that had beset Isabella ever since she had emerged from the icy stream. She towelled her body vigorously and set about getting dressed in the clothes that had been delivered to her room—plain, serviceable underclothing together with a woollen dress in a dull shade of brown.

She stood before the looking glass and inspected herself. Well, a dowdy dress was hardly going to help her look her best. She looked like a prim governess, if a little on the young side. That would never do. On impulse, she released the dark brown tresses from the bun at the back of her head, and brushed out her shoulder-length hair. She took a strand from each side and tied them loosely atop her head. There, that was better.

And why, pray, was she preening in front of a mirror and trying to look her best? Was it to impress that ogre of a man who had roared at her and lifted her off her horse as if she weighed little more than a feather? She shivered at the memory of his hands on her and the fire in his eyes as he had looked her over. No, this was ridiculous. She could not be having palpitations over Mr Wilson, the most uncouth man she had ever had the misfortune to meet.

Taking a deep breath, she composed herself. She would go down now and calmly explain to him what had happened down by the stream. And then she would smile politely and take her leave. There was no need to linger a minute longer than was necessary.

With a determined step, she made her way down to the parlour. She knocked on the door softly and walked into the room to find a subdued pair of children sitting with their heads bowed in remorse while they listened to their father's castigating diatribe. Mr Wilson paused his speech upon her entry into the room and turned to greet her.

"Miss Stanton, do come in and sit by the fire," he said in a deep, gravelly voice.

She went to the armchair by the hearth and sat as directed, expecting Mr Wilson to resume his lecture. He surprised her instead and came towards where she sat, looming over her with a frown creasing his brow. "Are you quite warm, Miss Stanton or do you still feel a chill?" he asked gruffly.

Something in the fierce manner with which he regarded her brought a tremble to her body. His eagle eyes did not miss the quiver of her hands, folded neatly in her lap. Before she knew it, he had taken them into his own, much larger ones. Isabella stared at him dazedly as he rubbed her hands between his, imparting heat and a sizzling current of electricity to every nerve in her body. Time stood still as all her attention was fixed on that point of contact between them, on the warm heat of his hands enveloping hers.

Eventually, he stopped the rubbing motion but did not let go of her hands. In a husky voice loaded with feeling, he said, "Miss Stanton, I am forever in your debt. If you had not happened to pass by when you did, I dread to think what would have become of Samuel. Thank you for saving him." Still, he held her hands.

Isabella could not look away from the brilliance of his eyes, nor could she think clearly while he continued to sear her with his touch. She stumbled on her words. "I, yes it was fortunate I came upon them. I did what anyone would have done."

"Not anyone. I can think of a fair few ladies that would have baulked at the idea of jumping into an icy stream to rescue a child." As if suddenly aware that he was still holding on to her hands, he let go abruptly and stepped away. "Samuel!" he barked as he went to sit. "What do you have to say?"

The small boy looked shyly in her direction. "Thank you, Miss Stanton, for rescuing me," he said in a small voice.

"What else?" prompted his father.

"I am so very sorry," said Samuel, hunching down in his seat.

He looked so woebegone that Isabella felt quite sorry for him, despite the fact he had evidently done wrong. "Your apology is accepted, Samuel," she said to him with a smile. "Let it be a lesson though to never venture out without an adult to look after you."

"It won't happen again, will it, Samuel?" demanded Mr Wilson.

"No, sir," responded the young boy.

Isabella thought it prudent to now make her excuses and take her leave. She rose to her feet. "Well, now that is all sorted, I had best be on my way," she said, putting on a jovial smile.

"You are going nowhere, Miss Stanton, until you have partaken of luncheon with us," insisted Mr Wilson.

"Oh no, that is quite alright," demurred Isabella. "They shall wonder what has become of me if I do not return home soon."

Mr Wilson was on his feet and staring at her again with that intense look that made her insides quiver. "No, they will not," he said in that deep voice. "I sent word that you shall be having luncheon with us, though I did not care to worry your family by informing them of your mishap. They will not expect you home until later in the afternoon, when I shall escort you there myself in my carriage."

"My—my horse," was all Isabella could think to say.

"Has already been dispatched to your home with one of my grooms. Rest easy, Miss Stanton. All is in hand."

Isabella hovered uncertainly. She really could not stay. Good gracious, she did not even like this man. Why on earth would she endure his hospitality a minute longer than necessary?

"That is very kind of you, Mr Wilson, but really, I must be going," she said rather breathlessly.

Now he stepped towards her, his powerful body so close that his male scent invaded her senses. He merely said one word. "Stay."

And that one word was enough. Her feet froze in place, as if indeed he were a magician, casting a spell on her to stay. She still thought she ought to go, but her feet refused to uphold her will. She caught then the curious stares of the two young children in the room with them and felt herself flush. "Very well," she mumbled and sank back down into her chair.

The spell broken, Mr Wilson stepped away. An awkward silence ensued as he took his seat. Instinctively, Isabella knew that he was not one for casual chit chat. Neither was she. Desperately, she scrambled for something to say, eventually coming up with, "I hope you are comfortably settled in Netherwick Hall."

He nodded. "We are."

"I suppose this must be quite a change to your old life in Manchester," she went on resolutely.

"Yes, it is."

Oh dear, this conversation was not going anywhere. Succour came from an unlikely direction. Theodora spoke up, "I like it much better here!"

"Me too," concurred Samuel.

"And me," added Mr Wilson, "so that makes it unanimous."

Isabella smiled. "I'm glad. I too am rather fond of this place."

"Did you grow up here?" asked Theodora.

"No, actually I grew up in a place called Ohio, in America."

"America!" exclaimed the children in awe.

"That would explain the hint of an accent I detected in your speech," mused Mr Wilson.

"I have lived in England for two years now, so my American speech has faded, but I am sure a hint of it lingers still."

"Do explain if you please, Miss Stanton," said Mr Wilson examining her with a frown, "how you came to live in America."

Isabella laughed. "It is quite simple really. Many years ago, my father and uncle decided to go to America and make their fortune there. They claimed land in Ohio, spent years clearing and cultivating it, and built themselves each a fine house to boot."

She could tell Mr Wilson was puzzled. "But they already had a great fortune here in England."

"My grandfather was rich as Croesus," corrected Isabella. "Unfortunately, there was a falling out between them, mostly to do with Papa's decision to marry my mother, whom Grandfather disapproved of."

"I see. And how came you to return?"

"We were summoned back here when Grandfather became sick," she explained. "And after he passed, the Stanton estate was divided between myself, my older brother and two cousins. Netherwick Hall and the surrounding farmland was my share of the inheritance."

"And so you stayed on here to take charge of your estate," guessed Mr Wilson.

"That's right," bristled Isabella. "I am as capable as any male in my family to manage my own affairs."

"You are very young," Mr Wilson pointed out.

"And what is that to mean?"

He raised a brow. "Only that you are very young."

"I am of age, and that is quite old enough, I assure you. I have managed quite well these past two years."

He surprised her then. "I was the same age when I set up my first factory," he said, sounding amused, "so I can hardly cast any stones."

Now it was Isabella's turn to exclaim, "You opened a factory when you were twenty-two? But that is very young!"

He laughed out loud. "It would seem we are both extremely precocious, Miss Stanton."

They were interrupted then by the arrival of a servant to announce that luncheon was served. With a most pleasing manner, Mr Wilson escorted her to the dining room. Perhaps he was not as uncouth as she had first thought. Could she have been too hasty in her judgement? Then she reminded herself of an important fact. He had made his fortune through the sweat and toil of the unfortunate workers in his factories, and no doubt his mills were in full collusion with the cotton plantation owners of the American south, putting money into the coffers of the very people fighting against her brother. Stiffly, she took her seat at the dining table, fully resolved to maintain a haughty distance from this bewildering man.

Chapter 7

Silas

That cool, haughty look had returned to Miss Stanton's countenance. He was not sure what he could have done to earn the young lady's disdain. He had thought on their first meeting that she objected to him on snobbish principles—not being of the gentlemanly class to which she was accustomed.

But after their talk and his discovery that her father had made his fortune through the toil of his hands in America, he could not quite believe that Miss Stanton would object to his own history. Something else irked her about him, but he was damned if he knew what. And really, did it matter? He was not about to act on the strange attraction that had risen up in him for this chit of a girl. Better indeed to keep a cold distance.

The soup was served, and he was pleased to see Miss Stanton eat it all up, a healthy colour returning to her cheeks. They addressed few words to one another during the meal. Fortunately, the children—now recovered from their ordeal—filled the gap in the conversation with their ebullient chatter. They quizzed Miss Stanton about everything under the moon—her favourite books, whether it was ever acceptable to put mustard in a sandwich, the merits of spiced cakes over iced buns—and she responded with an easy friendliness that soon had Theodora and Samuel won over, himself too.

After the soup came a serving of delicately steamed salmon served with a white sauce and green beans. Silas watched Miss Stanton like a hawk as she took a first helping of the fish. A smile came upon her face. "Mmm," she murmured appreciatively. "This is very good."

Silas sent a silent blessing to Mrs Jones, vowing to reward her with an increase in wages for this meal alone. The children ate hungrily and continued their happy chatter with Miss Stanton, whose first name, he discovered, was Isabella. *Isabella.* He tried the name out in his head. It suited her.

"You must get your father to take you to the Michaelmas Fair," Isabella was saying. "It is held in two weeks' time and promises to be lots of fun. There'll be music, dancing, and stalls selling all sorts of things."

"Oh, do please let's go!" pleaded Theodora.

"Yes, say we'll go, Papa," Samuel added his plea to the mix.

"I am not minded to reward your behaviour today," he replied sternly. At their dispirited sighs, he relented. "Let us see how we go on these next two weeks. I want to hear glowing reports of your studies with Miss Grainger, and absolutely no more disobedience."

"We'll be as good as gold," promised Theodora.

"You won't be disappointed," added Samuel.

Silas regarded his children with fond amusement but contented himself with saying, "We shall see."

The following course was served, a game pie with glazed carrots and roasted parsnips. Silas saw to it that a generous portion was plated up for his guest. Again, he watched her carefully as she took her first taste of the pie. Though she did not say anything, it seemed to her liking, and she ate a healthy quantity of it. So too did his children, their adventure today seemingly having heightened their appetite. Silas relaxed in his seat, thankful and glad that life had blessed him with the ability to provide generously for his family and guests. It was a far cry from the simple suppers he had eaten as a child.

Next up was a finely sliced sirloin of beef with an aromatic gravy, accompanied by sauteed potatoes and a side helping of creamed spinach. Isabella looked upon it in surprise, exclaiming, "Why this luncheon is more like a feast!"

Silas felt a swell of pleasure and pride, although this was rapidly punctured a moment later by Samuel innocently explaining, "We do not usually eat like this, Miss Stanton. It is all because of you being here."

"Oh," murmured Isabella, a spot of colour on her cheeks. "There was no need to go to all this trouble just for me."

"It was no trouble," Silas stated firmly, though Mrs Jones no doubt might have disagreed.

He continued to observe Isabella as she sliced the beef on her plate and tasted her first bite. "Perfectly tender," she praised. "Please send my compliments to your cook."

He would be sure to do so. Mrs Jones would be glad to hear that her efforts had been well appreciated. Silas had found it good practice in all his dealings both with household staff and factory workers to lavish praise where it was due. People were almost always willing to go the extra mile if their endeavours were acknowledged and valued. That and getting well paid, of course.

Silas had been fortunate at his factories to avoid the labour strikes that had plagued others, and he put it down to the fairness with which he treated all his workers. It made sense for him to pay a decent wage and provide good working conditions. In return, he avoided disruption to his business through sickness and strikes, gained productive work and made a tidy profit in the bargain. In his view, it did not make good business sense to cut corners, as many other industrialists often did.

His musings were brought to a halt when Theodora said most earnestly, "Do come and dine with us more often, Miss

Stanton. We shall get to feast like this and moreover, you are splendid company."

Isabella laughed. "I am not sure which it is you like more, Theo, the food or my company." The latter, most definitely, thought Silas, conscious of a feeling of lightness in his being that he had not felt in a very long time, if ever. Isabella's earlier stiff demeanour was gone, replaced by friendly good humour and, if he was not mistaken, a thrumming awareness of the attraction blossoming between them. It was not one-sided, this attraction. He was too experienced to misread Isabella's response to him. He did not miss the surreptitious glances she cast his way whenever she thought he was not looking. Oh, dear Lord, it was going to take a monumental effort to resist Isabella Stanton, especially when he knew with every fibre of his being that she wanted him too.

Chapter 8

Isabella

Isabella was back in the pink damask room. A knock at the door heralded the entrance of a maid, bearing her clothes which had been meticulously washed and pressed. Isabella smiled pleasantly at her. "Thank you," she said, taking hold of her dress and examining it. "You have done a wonderful job with it. I am truly grateful."

"It was no trouble, miss," replied the maid.

"Oh, I am sure it was," laughed Isabella, "especially in so short a time." Then she asked, "What is your name?"

"Nellie, miss."

"Well, Nellie, let me give you something for your troubles." Isabella reached over for her reticule and pulled open the drawstring.

"Oh, no, miss," protested Nellie. "I could not take anything. It would not be right."

"Why not? I am sure Mr Wilson badgered you into getting this task done quickly when you must have had lots of other, more important things to do. It is only right I reward you for your troubles."

Nellie looked shocked. "No, miss. That is not how it is. Mr Wilson is kindness itself and would never badger any of us. And truly, I do not need a reward. Mr Wilson promised I could take the day off on Saturday for having done a good job on the dress."

Isabella put her reticule back down. "I see," she said. "Well in that case, I hope you enjoy your time off, and thank you, Nellie."

The maid bobbed a curtsy then hurried out of the room. Alone again, Isabella pondered this new information about Mr Wilson as she dressed in her freshly pressed clothes. It had been a surprise to hear him described as "kindness itself", yet on further reflection, she conceded that he had been nothing but kind to her ever since she had arrived in his home today. She did not know quite what to make of it all.

She smoothed the skirt of her dress down with hands that shook slightly. It was all because of that impossible man. She'd had every intention to freeze him off, but it had been very difficult to do when he had fed her so well—that lemon tart had been divine—and his children had managed to charm her with their joyful zest for life. And then there was him…

Throughout the meal, she had felt his presence, looming larger than life. He spoke little, but when he did, she felt the resonance of his voice in every part of her being. She could not help casting curious glances at him whenever he wasn't looking. He was not handsome, not like her brother or Mr Templeton were, the two most eligible men in the county. The planes of his face were hewn a little too harshly for beauty. There was a silvery scar that ran down his upper lip, giving him a faintly raffish look. Be that as it may, she could not keep her eyes away. Something drew her back each and every time. It was becoming increasingly difficult to remember why she should dislike this man.

And now, he was to take her back home in his carriage. She would be alone with him in that confined space for an hour's journey. Dear Lord, how was she to maintain her composure and her distance for all that time? She would have to try her best. Mr Wilson, as fascinating as he might be, was not for her.

He was too old, for one thing—at least a dozen years her senior. And she should not forget that he was a factory owner, with all the misery that entailed. She would stand firm on her principles, yes she would.

After casting one last look at herself in the mirror, she made her way down to the entrance hall where Mr Wilson had said he would wait for her. She found him sitting at a chair by the hearth, perusing a newspaper. He set it down immediately upon seeing her and stood. She felt his disconcerting gaze on her and the corresponding upbeat of her heart. *"Stand firm, Isabella,"* she reminded herself. She gave him a cool smile as she placed her hand lightly on his arm and allowed him to escort her to the waiting carriage.

Once she was comfortably ensconced inside, Mr Wilson knocked on the roof with his stick to instruct the coachman to start their journey. He settled himself beside her, and for several minutes, silence reigned between them as the carriage began to move at a smart pace. Although it was a cool, cloudy day, she felt the heat emanating from his powerful frame sitting in such close proximity. She was engulfed once more by his scent—a lemony cologne entwined with a male musk that was making her feel quite dizzy.

The silence between them lengthened. She could think of nothing to say and, so it seemed, neither could he. Loud within this silence was the pounding of her unruly heart as well as a nearly tangible buzz of electricity in the air between them. Isabella took shallow, panting breaths, trying unsuccessfully to calm her racing heart. From the corner of her eye, she saw his hand curl up into a fist, as if he were exerting a supreme effort to control some raging impulse.

"Isabella," he grunted.

"Yes, Mr Wilson?" she breathed.

"Call me Silas," came the gruff reply. *Silas*. Of course, no other name would do for him.

"Silas," she whispered.

"Dear Lord!" he exclaimed. Next moment, she was in his arms and his lips were on hers. He claimed her in a brutal kiss, unrelenting in its ardour. Caught unawares, her hands at first flailed helplessly in the air before landing in the soft silk of his hair. Exquisite sensation assailed her from the warm, soft feel of his lips, the roughness of the whiskers on his jaw, the intoxication of his scent.

He held her tight to him, and through the layers of fabric, she felt the heat and power of his body. Next moment, his velvet tongue stroked her lips, coaxing them to part and allow him to enter her mouth. Good gracious! She had never dreamed that kissing could be an intimate invasion like this. It left her reeling. She knew now the unique taste of him, and she did not think she could ever stop her craving for it.

Time stood still as he kissed her, and she kissed him back with growing hunger. She could not tell how long their lips were locked in this passionate embrace. It seemed an eternity yet also not nearly long enough. She wanted more. More of what, she could not articulate, but simply more. A deep well of need had arisen inside her. She arched against him and moaned the urgency of her want. He seemed to understand, for he wrenched his lips from hers and commenced a journey with his mouth along her jaw and the sensitive column of her throat. She trembled with each touch and moaned, "Silas, oh Silas."

"Bella," he groaned, returning to drop endless kisses on her lips.

Isabella felt her entire body throb with an unresolved ache. She was a quivering mass of need, barely able to think clearly. All she could do was stare into the dark pools of his eyes. "Please, Silas," she whimpered, not knowing exactly what she was pleading for. But it seemed he knew. Heat flared in his dark eyes as he lifted the ends of her skirt, burrowing his hand underneath. His eyes never left her face as his hand crept slowly up her thigh and inched towards that most private part of her. He found the slit of her drawers and slipped his fingers inside. She trembled in reaction when a moment later, his fingers touched her there. "Oh," she cried.

He stared at her, a frown of intense concentration on his face as his fingers began to stroke her in that intimidate place. She ought to put a stop to this depravity, but she could not, for it was too good. This, she realised, was what she had instinctively begged for, and now he was giving her what she craved. On and on he stroked, studying every changing expression on her face as he did so. Glorious sensation was building at her core, a maelstrom that grew and grew in intensity until she thought she could bear it no more.

"That's it, Bella," he rasped. "Let it happen."

And then it did. Pulses of exquisite pleasure ripped through her. For endless seconds, she was gripped in a paroxysm of sensation. When finally, it was over, she found herself tucked into Silas's embrace, his hand stroking her gently. She closed her eyes and gave in to a pleasant lassitude. With her face nestled to his chest, she felt the comforting beat of his heart.

It took some time for rational thought to return. As it did, she felt herself stiffen in his arms, horror seeping in at what she had just done. All at once, she pushed him away with as much force as she could muster. He grunted in displeasure but did not resist, dropping his arms and letting her go. For a few heartbeats, they sat rigidly apart from one another, not speaking. Then, Isabella gathered the courage to say, "I do not know what came over me, but I hope, sir, that we can put this unfortunate episode behind us and never speak of it again."

"Bella," he rumbled. "Do shut up."

"I beg your pardon!" she cried in indignation.

"If you are going to speak abject nonsense, then it is better you do not speak at all."

"Well," spluttered Isabella, "if you are going to be rude, then it is better *you* do not speak at all."

He ran an irritated hand through his hair and growled, "How else would you have me respond to your telling me that the best kiss I have ever had was an 'unfortunate episode' never to be spoken of again."

"Was it really that?" she asked hopefully.

"By far," he stated firmly, "just as it was the best you ever had too."

She huffed. "Actually, it was the only kiss I've ever had."

His expression softened. "Then that was quite the introduction to kissing." After a pause, he added, "Was it also your first orgasm?"

At her puzzled look, he expounded, "An orgasm is that state of pleasurable completion you experienced as I stroked you, Bella. It will have felt like rippling convulsions at the core of your body."

"Oh," she said, feeling her face flame at the memory.

"Was it your first time?" he asked softly.

"Well, of course it was. You must know I have never been with a man like this before."

He chuckled. "I have it on good authority that a lady can achieve an orgasm without the assistance of a man."

She was suddenly full of raging jealousy. "On whose authority?" she demanded.

She wished then that she had not asked, for the smile was wiped off his face as he said, "Ada. My wife."

She looked away, asking under her breath, "When did she pass?"

"Just over nine months ago," he said in a hoarse voice.

"Did you—did you love her very much?" she asked quietly.

At first, he did not answer. Then, on a deep exhale of his breath, he said, "I do not think it right to speak of Ada after what we have just done, but yes, I did love her."

His words sent an unexpected shard of jealousy into her heart. She nodded and said with determination, "It is best then we do not speak of this again. We will put the whole thing behind us."

His expression hardened. "We will do no such thing."

Instinctively, she lashed back, still under the influence of that green-eyed monster. "The only thing worse than a mistake, sir, is to compound the mistake by repeating it. Quite clearly, we should not have kissed. You are still mourning your wife and much too old for me, beside which, I do not even like you."

"You seemed to like me well enough a few minutes ago," he snarled.

"Sir!" Isabella protested, appalled that he would be so indelicate as to bring up their recent indiscretion.

"What? Does it offend your sensibilities, Bella, to be reminded of the passion we shared?"

She held her head up high and sniffed, "A gentleman would never speak of it."

"Ah, but we both know I am no gentleman."

"All the more reason why there cannot be anything more between us," she declared.

Silas regarded her with derision. "Careful, Bella, your true snobbish colours are showing."

"I am not a snob!" she cried, much offended.

"No? I can hardly think of another reason why you have held your pretty nose up in the air at me from the first we met."

Isabella gathered herself up haughtily. "Perhaps, sir," she said in frigid tones, "it has to do with the fact you have enriched yourself at the expense of the poor workers in your factories, and that your cotton mills are in connivance with the slave plantations of the American south."

"You do not know what you talk of," he bit back, a scowl marring his face.

"Do I not?" she retorted. "I know that my brother at this very moment is risking his life in a war against the Confederacy, whose weapons are in part funded by the cotton trade—by factories such as yours."

He pinched the sleeve of her dress between his thumb and forefinger, and leaned so close that she could see the black irises of his eyes. "If we are to talk about connivance with the slave trade," he hissed, "then there is no finer example than this cotton here with which your dress is made. And how about all the underclothes made from cotton that the fine folk of this country slip on each day? Are they also to be considered complicit in slavery?"

To this, she had no answer. It was true that cotton clothing was everywhere to be found, and every penny spent on such clothing was indirectly funding the Confederacy's slave plantations. But what were people to do? Wear only silk or scratchy wool for their underclothes? She could find no easy answers to that conundrum.

He watched her grapple with this vexed question, and his lips curled. "No answer to that, have we? Well now, let me correct some of your assumptions about me, not that I am under any obligation to explain myself to you. Firstly, the cotton used in my mills comes mostly from Egypt, not America. And secondly, I did not enrich myself at the expense of my workers. They all got paid a very fair wage, many of them being lifted out of the poverty you so decry through their work in my factories."

The carriage had come to a halt at the front entrance of Stanton Hall. Silas cast a glance out through the window then turned his attention back to her. "But fear not," he said with a sardonic twist to his lips. "I will relieve you of my offending presence very shortly." So saying, he opened the carriage door and jumped down. With exaggerated courtesy, he handed her down and bowed. "Good day, Miss Stanton."

Mutely, she curtsied. Then, without another word, she ran up the steps and past the butler, who held the front door open for her. She did not stop until she reached the haven of her room. There, she threw herself on the bed and burst into unremitting sobs.

Chapter 9

Silas

For the rest of the day, Silas stewed over Isabella's words. He did not know why they had wounded him so deeply. He told himself she was but an ignorant, foolish girl, and he had long ago learned not to care too deeply about what other people thought of him. Why should he care now?

But care he did. It was all to do with this burgeoning attraction he had for her—one that needed to be very quickly nipped in the bud. There was no place in his life for a hoity-toity young miss who looked down her nose at him.

He sighed now as he got into his bed and arranged the pillows at his side. His eyes lingered on them wryly. What a sad state of affairs that he had to clutch a pillow at night in order not to feel so alone. Perhaps his sister was right, and he needed to remarry; not some haughty chit of a girl, but a lady of mature years who could provide companionship and help ease the ache of loneliness.

He settled under the covers and extinguished the light, promising himself that first thing tomorrow, he would write to his sister to arrange a visit. She would be sure, he knew, to engineer some meeting with the lady she had in mind for him. It was not a prospect he relished, but he would have to grit his teeth and endure it.

He closed his eyes and tried to sleep, yet his thoughts kept returning to that carriage ride today with Isabella—the unforgettable kiss, watching her face as she spent under the touch of his fingers, and then their bitter argument afterwards.

He should have realised, when earlier she had talked of growing up in Ohio, that her family would somehow be embroiled in the war that raged in America at this time. Of course, she would be partisan in favour of the Union, what with her brother being a soldier in its army. Silas himself had no great allegiance to either side, though he had no love for slavery. His overriding concern was that war was bad for business, and the sooner the conflict was brought to a close, the better. But, of course, it was different for Isabella. Chief among her concerns would be the safety of her family.

He considered the matter from another perspective. If it were Samuel years from now fighting in a war, how would Silas feel about the people on the other side of the conflict? Deep animosity? Most likely. It was not too much of a stretch for him to imagine how Isabella must feel about the Confederacy and any entity that supported it. He well knew that some unscrupulous mill owners were finding ways to break the blockade of ships in the Atlantic in order to get their hands on the precious commodity they needed for their factories, in some cases shipping weapons to the Confederacy in exchange for shipments of cotton. It had been unfair of Isabella to tar him with the same brush but understandable, he supposed.

Still, he had not liked being judged so by her, and he had needed to set the record straight. Whether his words had had any effect, he did not know. He was not about to go calling upon her to find out. Painful as this was, he told himself it was for the best. They would go their separate ways, and he would endeavour to wean himself of the inconvenient feelings he had developed for Miss Isabella Stanton.

He shifted in the bed, trying to get comfortable, then turned on his side, throwing his right arm and leg over the mound of pillows, as if they were a real person there with him. He did not dream of Ada though, nor of some imaginary female he might one day marry. No, his thoughts strayed to Bella. If it were her in his arms right now, his hand would wander over her body, getting a good feel of her delightful breasts. He would nibble at the sensitive line of her throat as he slipped his fingers down to her pleasure spot and stroked her to completion. Only then would he lay her beneath him so he could drive his hard cock over and over into her tight heat, until he spent his seed deep within her.

All this was fantasy, of course, except for one part. His cock was rock hard and leaking at the tip, such was his need. It had been a long time since he had lain with a woman—nearly ten months in fact. He had been faithful to Ada all the years of their marriage, and to her memory after she passed. For months, these natural urges had been subsumed in the numbness of grief. Now, they burst into life again.

Silas turned onto his back and took hold of his engorged shaft. Spreading the wetness from the tip to the rest of his length, he began to pleasure himself with rapid strokes of his hand. It was not long before he reached a powerful climax and spurted his release. He lay spent for a few moments, then reached in the dark for his discarded shirt, using it to wipe off the stickiness of his seed. Then, he slumped back in the bed and soon after was claimed by blessed sleep.

Next morning, he sent off a note to his sister and summoned Miss Grainger for stern words at having left the children unattended the previous day. These duties fulfilled, and having spent some time with his two young progeny at breakfast, he set out for the stable to get his horse. It had been a week since they had moved into Netherwick Hall, during which time he had been busy settling in. Now, he felt the need to explore further afield and become acquainted with his neighbours. He liked to know all the people that lived in his vicinity, in all the classes of the social order. There were several farms hereabouts, all tenants of Isabella Stanton. He would visit them and make himself known, even though he did not have any particular business with anyone, after which he would continue on to the village and pay a call on the establishments there.

He headed east, planning to take a circular route around Netherwick Hall. First, he passed a field laid to grass on which cattle grazed placidly. Next he came upon some labourers harvesting a field of turnips. He stopped briefly and spoke to them. To his enquiries, they replied that these fields were part of the Flint farm and that Farmer Flint himself was busy in the next field supervising the loading of wheat sheaves onto his wagons. Silas thanked them and went on his way, soon locating Mr Flint.

He dismounted his horse, and keeping the reins in his hand, approached the farmer. "Good day, sir," he said by way of greeting. "Looks to me like a mighty fine harvest is to be had this year."

"Aye," replied the farmer. "Reckon it's the best in two decades and more. And who might you be, sir, if you pardon my asking?"

"I am Silas Wilson, newly of Netherwick Hall."

"Ah," said Mr Flint knowledgeably. "You be the mill owner from up north."

Silas chuckled. His reputation had indeed preceded him. "That I am," he said. "And you must be Mr Flint."

"You have the right of it, sir."

Silas looked about him keenly. As far as the eye could see were acres of neatly harvested fields with sheaves of wheat and barley stacked into pyramid-like stooks for drying. These would soon be loaded onto wagons to be taken to the stackyard. "I can see you shall be kept quite busy loading up all these stooks," he said by way of conversation.

"It is a busy time of the year, but if the weather holds, we shall soon be done with it," replied the farmer. "Can't be saying the same about the Shaws," he added with a snort. "Bad business that is, very bad business." He shook his head in disgust.

"The Shaws?" enquired Silas mildly.

"The smallholding neighbouring mine, sir, farmed by the Shaws. A very sad state of affairs," grimaced Mr Flint.

Silas felt a pique of interest. "How so?" he wondered out loud.

Mr Flint chose to answer this question with a query of his own. "I suppose you have met Miss Stanton, she who owns this land and Netherwick Hall. What did you think of the lady?"

Silas was not about to enlighten the farmer as to his true thoughts about Isabella. "She is young," he replied noncommittally.

That was a statement of fact, not an opinion, though Mr Flint chose to take it as such. "Aye," he said, with another shake of his head. "As I said, it is a sad state of affairs, this business with the Shaws, and Miss Stanton, no disrespect to the lady, is young and let herself be taken in by them. Such a very great pity, but what else can you expect when a young miss barely out of the schoolroom is put in charge of an estate?"

Silas's curiosity was now fully aroused. "Do explain yourself, Mr Flint," he said coolly. "What is this sad state of affairs you speak of?"

But the farmer would not be drawn any further. "It is not for me to say," he blustered. "I did offer my help after Shaw met his maker a fortnight ago, but Miss Stanton would not listen." He gave a voluble sigh. "The Shaws will be lucky to have their harvesting done before the rains come, that's all I have to say. Now if you'll excuse me, Mr Wilson, I had best be getting on with my own work." With a doff of his cap, Mr Flint walked off to mount the driver's seat of his loaded wagon then began leading it away.

Silas stood watching him disappear into the distance, eyes narrowed. What on earth had Isabella got herself entangled in? He needed to know. And if Mr Flint was not going to enlighten him, then he had best go to the source. Nimbly, he mounted his horse and began riding in the direction of the Shaw farm.

A short while later, he drew up by a field where he saw a group of people busily loading up a wagon with harvested sheaves of wheat. On closer inspection, the group consisted of three lads, the youngest perhaps no more than ten, and a woman of middle years, whose resemblance to the boys marked her out as their mother. To the eldest of the boys fell the job of lifting the heavy sheaves and heaving them onto the wagon, where the others pushed them into neat stacks, under the direction of the woman, who could be none other than Mrs Shaw.

Silas dismounted his horse and approached, calling out a greeting. They paused their travails and responded in kind. "Do I have the pleasure to address Mrs Shaw?" asked Silas.

"Yes, I am Mrs Shaw," said the woman, cautiously polite. "And your good self?"

Silas replied, "I am Silas Wilson, the new occupant of Netherwick Hall."

"The factory owner from up north?" asked one of the young lads.

His fame had spread far and wide it seemed. "Yes, that is me," confirmed Silas. Then he went straight to the point, as he liked to do. "I have just now spoken with Mr Flint of the neighbouring farm. He had some dire warnings to give about the state of your harvest. I came to find out how things are, as well as to make myself known to you."

At the sound of Mr Flint's name, Mrs Shaw's lips pursed. "Greedy Old Flint," she cursed under her breath.

Her son was more forthright. "That old crook!" he cried. "If we do not manage to get this harvest done in time, it will be all thanks to him."

"I was sorry to hear of the recent passing of Mr Shaw," said Silas gently. "Do accept my deepest condolences."

"Thank you, sir," responded Mrs Shaw with great dignity. "The matter put simply is this. Mr Flint has had his eye on our farm for quite some time, and when my husband passed away, he scented his opportunity. Straight to Miss Stanton he went, claiming that we could not manage the farm, given my eldest, Pete, is just sixteen. He gave her a cock and bull story about how the harvest would be at risk unless the farm was put in his name immediately."

Things were beginning to fall into place. Silas had met men of Mr Flint's ilk before. The world of business was full of cunning predators waiting to prey on the weak. He wondered how Isabella had responded to Mr Flint's nefarious overtures. He had to ask. "And what did Miss Stanton have to say to that?"

Mrs Shaw drew herself up proudly. "She came to see us the very next morning, and when I told her we could manage the farm with all of us pulling together to get the work done, she agreed to let us keep the land, but on condition we can prove to her within three months that we are up to the task of running the farm."

Here, Pete took on the rest of the tale. "Old Flint got wind of this, and ever since, has done everything in his power to hinder our efforts—make it seem to Miss Stanton we can't manage things. He's going around telling folk like your good self that our harvest is about to fail. Then, he made sure to hire all the spare labourers in the village. Now, we can't find anyone to help us get the work done. And that's not all. Just this morning, two of our cart horses were hobbled, most suspiciously I should say, leaving us with just this one here to pull our wagon. It's going to slow us down quite a bit, as one horse alone cannot pull a heavy load." His face took on a bullish expression. "But we'll get the job done. I'll make sure of it."

Silas considered the matter and came to a quick decision. Unbuttoning his jacket and dropping it to the ground, he began rolling up the sleeves of his shirt. The Shaws observed him in stunned silence, not quite sure what to make of him. He looked up at them and raised a brow. "Well now," he said calmly, "it seems you have yourself an extra pair of hands and another horse. Phoenix here is not much used to pulling carts, but I am sure he'll manage. Let us get to work."

Chapter 10

Isabella

Isabella spent a troubled few days brooding over what had happened in that carriage journey with Silas Wilson. That kiss. The way he had touched her — down there — and then the harsh words that had been spoken afterwards. She winced at the memory of the things she had said.

She had accused him of exploiting his factory workers and colluding with the slave trade. Then she had gone on to claim that the guns pointed at her brother in battle were funded by factories such as his. Except that she had been wrong. Not for the first time in her life, she had rushed to judgement about someone and been horribly mistaken.

How was she ever to face him again after the things they had done and the accusations she had thrown at him? It all made for a most uncomfortable chain of thoughts. She was so distracted that even her older brother Daniel noticed, but he thankfully put it down to worry about Benjamin. Well, she did worry about him too, just one more thing to add to her pile of troubled musings. What would Daniel think if he knew the truth, that she was a brazen hussy who had allowed a man to touch her in a most intimate place and then compounded that behaviour by throwing unjust insults at him. Dear Lord, what a mess she had made of things.

On the third day of this state of affairs, she decided it was time to venture out again from the confines of Stanton Hall. She would go visit the Shaw farm and see how they were getting on with the harvest. If she happened upon Mr Wilson at some point in her journey, then all the better. Perhaps then she would have an opportunity to utter words of apology. With this in mind, she took a circuitous route, skirting very close to Netherwick Hall on her way, but if she had hoped to come upon Mr Wilson taking a walk in the vicinity of his home, she was sadly disappointed.

She reached the Shaw farm mid-morning and dismounted her horse, tethering it in the stable, then she set out on foot for the fields, looking for the Shaws. As she walked along, she was pleased to note several wheat and corn fields shorn of their crop, the harvesting complete. It seemed the Shaws, contrary to rumours being circulated, were doing just fine. She felt a moment of relief, glad that the trust she had put in Mrs Shaw had not been misplaced.

After a few minutes' walk, she finally came upon the Shaws working busily in a field. The younger ones were gathering the sheaves of wheat and bringing them to where a wagon and two horses were being loaded up with the harvest. A man was hefting the wheat onto the wagon, his back turned to her. She perceived Mrs Shaw up above him on the wagon, arranging the sheaves into neat stacks.

For a minute or two, Isabella stood, observing them work. Her eyes were drawn towards the man, who wore a loose shirt with the sleeves rolled up to the elbows, exposing strong forearms, lightly tanned by the sun. Something about the man's broad muscularity seemed familiar. Who was he? Isabella stared as he bent and picked up the bunches of wheat then lifted them into the wagon with powerful grace.

Mrs Shaw was the first to notice her presence. She paused her work and called out, "Miss Stanton. Good day."

Isabella was about to respond when the man finally turned and faced her. She took in a sharp breath. It was Silas. For what seemed an eternity, Isabella gaped in his direction, unable to speak. A sheen of sweat was on his brow. His dark hair was mussed and windblown. Her gaze trailed down to his chest and took in the rippled muscles covered with a dusting of dark hair, visible through the buttons undone at the collar of his shirt. When her eyes travelled back up to his face, it was to see him scowling at her. This was the impetus she needed to finally emerge from her trance.

Shakily, she returned Mrs Shaw's greeting then turned her attention back to Silas. "Mr Wilson," she said in as calm a voice as she could manage. She was about to ask what he was doing here, but that would have been silly. It was quite obvious what he was doing. Instead, she said, "I had not thought to see you here, sir."

His lips curled into a sneer as he bit out, "Have I not told you before, Miss Stanton, that I am no gentleman? I am not too proud to work with the two hands the good Lord gave me."

But this time, Isabella would not be drawn into an argument. Instead, she said in a stilted voice, "It is very kind of you to help out the Shaws."

"That it is," agreed Mrs Shaw, joining the conversation. "We are mighty grateful to Mr Wilson for all his help."

"I was pleased to see just how much has been achieved since I was last here, Mrs Shaw," continued Isabella. "Do you think you will be able to get the harvest in before the weather turns?"

"Oh aye, we shall get it done, God willing," replied Mrs Shaw. "If you will excuse us, Miss Stanton, we had best be getting on with it."

"Of course," murmured Isabella, her eyes back on Silas whose fierce stare was making her quiver in remembrance of what they had done in the carriage. She ought to be heading back to her horse, her mission accomplished. Except she had yet to speak to Silas and apologise. A wild idea began to form in her head. If Silas was helping out in the fields to get the harvest in, then why could she not do so too? It was not as if she had never done such things before. Back home in Ohio, it had been all hands on deck at harvest time. It was only once she had come to England that she had lived the life of a lady of quality.

Quickly, she made her decision. Discarding her outer jacket and dropping it down, she announced, "I am sure an extra pair of hands would not go amiss." Then, she undid the fastenings at her wrist and rolled up the sleeves of her dress. She took a few steps forward until she was face to face with Silas, whose harsh stare had not faltered. In a low voice, she taunted, "Still think I'm a snob, Mr Wilson?"

All at once, his lips curved upwards into a wide grin. It quite transformed his face, making him seem years younger and almost handsome. "That's my girl," he rumbled approvingly. In an undertone, he added, "And Bella, it's Silas to you. Now go make yourself useful."

She almost took umbrage at the high-handedness of his tone, but she was too full of secret pleasure at having been called "my girl". With a flutter in the region of her heart, she turned and made her way along the field towards where the younger members of the Shaw family were gathering up the bundles of wheat. She joined them and began to pick up as many sheaves as she could carry in one go and taking them to the wagon. Each time she deposited her load at Silas's feet, she was rewarded with a smouldering look that brought more colour to her already rosy cheeks. However, he said nothing more and simply turned back to his task.

For the rest of the morning, she laboured along with the Shaws, going back and forth to the wagon, transporting the sheaves of wheat. What had at first seemed like easy work soon began to feel quite tiring, but Isabella persevered, refusing to show any sign of weakness. As long as everyone else was working industriously, she could not stop to rest. She wished she had something to drink though, as she was mightily thirsty, as well as hot and tired. With a sigh, she picked up her next load and began the arduous walk towards the wagon. When finally she reached it, she dropped the sheaves down with relief, sensing Silas's narrowed scrutiny. She gave him a faint smile before turning back to go gather more sheaves. He called out her name, halting her in her tracks. "Bella, come back here."

His tone was so authoritative that she obediently retraced her steps back to him, giving him an enquiring look. "Sit here," he grunted as he placed his hands at her waist and lifted her onto the edge of the wagon. A moment later, he had bent down to a small wooden barrel on the ground beside him and poured from it what looked like cider into a tankard. He held it up to her with the firm instruction, "Drink up."

She took the tankard from him with hands that shook slightly and brought it to her lips. She could feel his intense gaze fixed on her face as she drank. Once she was done, he took the tankard from her, but as she made to get down from the wagon, he barked out one word, "Stay." So, she stayed where she was, reflecting that it was getting quite commonplace for Silas to order her about, and wondering why it was she did not mind.

He bent down and refilled the tankard. "Would you like some more?" he asked. When she shook her head, he drank the contents himself, placing his lips on exactly the same spot where she had placed hers. She watched his throat work as he gulped down the liquid. He stood close, a hand placed only inches from her hip. She breathed in his scent, male and strong, and as her gaze met the brilliant black of his eyes, she felt a swirl of dizzy sensation. The world around them melted away. All she could see and sense was Silas.

In that instant, her body's core throbbed with that same deep ache she had experienced once before in the carriage. It was accompanied by a gush of wetness in her drawers. She took a deep, shuddering breath and murmured, "Silas."

He understood at once. Eyes burning with heat, he promised, "Oh Bella, I'll be taking care of you just as soon as we're done with the work here."

Her pulse leapt. There could be no doubting his intent. Did that also mean he had forgiven her? She had to speak now and tell him how sorry she was. "Silas," she said again, with a little more force. "I owe you an apology."

"No, Bella, you do not," he said bluntly. "I should have known, with your family being in America, how this war would be affecting you. I am sorry about your brother and pray that he is returned safely to you."

"But the accusations I threw at you—" she began.

"—were unjust and cut me to the quick," he said, completing her sentence. "It is understandable, though, how you might have reached those conclusions."

She had hurt him. She could read it clearly in his eyes. This fierce man with the commanding and at times brash manner had been wounded by her words. She marvelled that she had the power to affect him so, even as she felt stricken with regret. "Please forgive me," she begged softly.

"Always." His tone was gruff as he covered her hands with his. A moment later, he released her and stepped away. "We best get back to work," he said. "There is not much left of this field to do, after which, you will have your luncheon at Netherwick Hall." His voice brooked no dissent. She nodded meekly and allowed him to help her down to the ground. Slowly, she made her way back to where the younger Shaws were still busy gathering the wheat sheaves. For another hour or so, she worked away with them, returning to the wagon with her load and basking in Silas's attention each time she approached him. While she toiled, she thought of what he had said. *I'll be taking care of you just as soon as we're done with the work here.* Despite her growing fatigue, there was a tingle of anticipation within her breast. She was about to act like a hussy once more, and she could not seem to make herself care.

Though there was a question that went around in her mind as she gathered sheaves of wheat and walked with them to the wagon. Where was all this between her and Silas leading to? Was it just sport for him, a pleasurable dalliance to pass the time? Or was it something more?

She did not like to think of herself as someone who engaged in fleeting dalliances with men. She had never done anything of the sort before. There had been young bucks in Ohio who had flirted with her and might have taken things further had she not very correctly set them straight.

But this with Silas was different. He did not seem to be playing or flirting. More often than not, he watched her with a scowl or that fierce look upon his face, almost as if he did not wish to be attracted to her.

Then could this be something serious? Something that would lead to marriage?

Immediately, Isabella discarded the idea as ridiculous. Silas was still in the period of mourning for his wife, whom he had loved dearly by the sounds of it. He did not even like Isabella very much, despite the undoubted physical attraction between them. And then of course there was the age difference, not to mention the social gap between them. She was the daughter of an earl—and strictly speaking should go by the title of Lady Isabella Stanton though she preferred to be called Miss Stanton—whereas he was of far more humble origins. Such things might not matter much to her, having grown up in Ohio where her family's titles meant little, but it would cause ripples in society here. She had no wish to be the subject of gossip; her decision to take charge of her estate had caused enough eyebrows raised already.

Whichever way she looked at it, marriage to Silas Wilson seemed unlikely, which left only one thing on the table—an affair. For a short time, she let herself imagine it. There would be more of those dizzying kisses, and more touches down below leading to delightful orgasms. She would have the chance to run her hands down his body, touch his skin, breathe in his manly scent. Oh sweet Lord, that sounded fine! But what then? Affairs were by their nature short-lived, were they not? Eventually, theirs would end, and she would be left with the shame of having lain with a man. And she was quite sure that she would also be left with a broken heart.

No, an affair was out of the question too. She would have to stay firm and strong, and resist the pull this man was having on her. And the best way to do so was to avoid his company. She had better start on this path right away, for there was no time like the present.

When she reached the wagon with her load, she dropped it at Silas's feet then quickly turned to go retrieve her jacket from where she had left it on the ground. She pulled it on and pressed the buttons with hands that shook. Silas had stopped his work to level her with one of his ferocious stares. She ignored it determinedly. As soon as her jacket was buttoned up, she smiled vaguely in his direction and called out, "Good day." Then she turned and began to stride, as fast as she could, in the direction of the Shaw stable where she had left her horse.

She had barely made it to the edge of the field when Silas caught up with her, thundering, "Where do you think you're going?"

She did not slow her steps nor look in his direction. "I am going to fetch my horse, Mr Wilson," she replied primly, "and then I shall be riding home."

"The hell you are!" He caught her by the arm and forced her to stop, turning her to face his angry countenance. "What in the world do you think you're doing, Bella?" he rasped furiously.

Oh, he would not browbeat her. She straightened her spine and shot back, "I am doing the sensible thing, Mr Wilson, and returning home before temptation has us do something that we both know we should not do."

He growled in frustration, "I am growing tired of your blowing hot and cold, Bella."

"I am sorry for it," she said stiffly. "But if you think on the matter rationally, you will see that I am doing the right thing. This attraction between us can only lead to a tawdry affair." Her voice broke a little as she added, "And that I have not the stomach for." She snatched her arm from his grasp and began to walk in the direction of the stable once more.

He matched her step for step. Eventually, he spoke in a low, raspy voice. "Is that what you think it would be? A tawdry affair?"

She shrugged as she walked on. "What else could it be? After all, it cannot be marriage."

"Marriage!" he huffed, adding more quietly, "Of course not."

His confirmation of her earlier thoughts merely exacerbated the pain she was beginning to feel in the region of her heart. She had been right. He had no thought to ever marry her. They were so clearly mismatched. This for him was merely a carnal affair, but she knew this would never be enough for her. The pain strengthened her determination. She quickened her steps, wanting to be on her way home as soon as it was possible.

He kept up with her, not speaking, though a quick glimpse at his face confirmed his customary scowl was back in place. They arrived at the stable and entered together. As Isabella went to release her horse and lead it out, she saw Silas follow suit, bringing out his own horse, which she had not noticed when she had arrived earlier.

She led her horse to the mounting block and nimbly got on. Only then, did she look across at Silas, who was astride his own mount. "I will bid you good day, Mr Wilson," she said with as much dignity as she could muster.

He made a snorting sound but did not respond. With a flick of her rein, she began the journey home, Silas riding quietly beside her. When they reached the entrance to Netherwick Hall, she expected him to bid her farewell and turn in the direction of his home, but he kept riding along with her. Puzzled, she pulled on the reins to stop and turned to him. "Mr Wilson, I believe you have missed your turning."

"Miss Stanton," he returned coldly. "I may not be the gentleman you desire, but even I know the right thing is to see you home safely."

"There is no need," she protested. "I am quite used to riding on my own."

"I am coming with you like it or not," he said sharply. "Now we had best be getting along before you faint with hunger." With that, he urged his horse onwards, and reluctantly, so did she.

They rode the journey to Stanton Hall without another word. On arrival there, Silas stayed long enough to see her dismount and hand over her horse to a waiting groom. With a nod of his head, he bade her, "Good day, Miss Stanton," then was on his way again.

Chapter 11

Silas

"And how are you liking it at Netherwick Hall, Mr Wilson?" The question was asked by Mrs Corbett, who sat across from him at his sister's dinner table. It was Saturday, two days after the debacle with Isabella Stanton, and Silas had been invited to luncheon at his sister's house in Oxford, where of course, Esther had obligingly arranged for Mrs Corbett, the solicitor's widow, to also be present.

He could not fault his sister. After all, it had been his letter to her last week that had precipitated this event. He needed to remarry—this much was now becoming clear. Silas was not made for the bachelor life. Even before his marriage to Ada, he had not had much time for liaisons with the opposite sex. He had been far too busy setting up his first factory and working all hours of the day to make it succeed.

Furthermore, it was not in his nature to play courtship games. He was the sort of person who liked to get straight to the matter at hand. When he had first met Ada, a shopkeeper's daughter, he had not beaten about the bush. He had liked her calm, kindly demeanour each time he had come to purchase goods at her father's shop, and he had soon decided that she would suit him admirably as a wife. On his next visit, he had taken her to one side and stated his intention to propose. She had promptly accepted. There had been no doubts or uncertainties with Ada. Their relationship had progressed smoothly from acquaintances to betrothal to marriage. And theirs had been a happy union.

All this was in stark contrast to his interactions with Isabella Stanton. For the first time in his life, he was riddled with uncertainty. Oh, he knew well enough that he desired her. That much had been clear from their first meeting. It was also becoming clear that what he felt for her was more than simply desire. Why else did she have the power to rattle him so, and even to wound him? For some unfathomable reason, her good opinion mattered to him. And here was the crux of his uncertainty, for she had made no bones of her disdain for him — even while quite plainly desiring him.

He had thought he could not be hurt any more than he already had been by her accusations of connivance with slavery, but her conviction that all they could ever have together was a tawdry affair had lanced him deeply. *After all, it cannot be marriage*, she had said with finality. In that moment, he had known two things — firstly, that he had indeed dreamed of making her his wife and secondly, that this dream had turned to ashes. She would not have him. The barrier of social class was insurmountable, so it seemed.

He had returned home in a shockingly bad temper and closeted himself away in his study. That night, he had slept restlessly, unable to stop thinking of Isabella Stanton. Why could he just not erase her from his mind? In the past, he had been prosaic about the battles he could win and those that he could not. His philosophy had always been that there was no point wasting time flogging a dead horse. If it was not to be, then it was not to be. Best to be moving on.

This was the reason why he had forced himself to sit at this luncheon and talk amiably with Violet Corbett. He was not made to be a bachelor, and Isabella Stanton quite clearly did not see him as a suitable prospect for matrimony. Therefore, he had better find himself another, more amenable lady to be his wife. Granted, he had been wary of the idea when his sister had first broached the matter to him. However, the more he tied himself in knots over Isabella Stanton, the more urgently he was gripped by the need to find an escape into calmer waters where he could return to his usual certainty. He trusted his sister's instincts. She was canny and wise when it came to people. She would not guide him wrong.

"I like it very well," he now replied to Mrs Corbett's query. "It is a little too fancy a place for a person such as me, but it has many charms, chief of which is the parkland. It is a much more pleasant place for my morning constitutional than I have been used to, living in Manchester."

"I can quite imagine," she smiled. "It will suit the needs of your children too, I should think, giving them more space to play outside in the fresh air."

"You are quite right," Silas smiled back. Mrs Corbett had a thoughtful, quiet manner and a pleasant demeanour. It was no fault of hers, of course, that she was not Isabella Stanton.

"We should organise a visit," stated Esther decisively. "Silas, why don't you host a weekend party at Netherwick Hall? We could do it the weekend after the Michaelmas Fair." She cast him a long look, making it plain she expected him to agree.

The thought of his home being overrun with guests was not a happy one, but he understood well enough that this would be an opportunity for him to have private discourse with Violet Corbett and to move this courtship forward. At this inopportune moment, Isabella came to his mind once more. A voice in his head said quite insistently that it was her he wished to court, not anyone else. With an effort, he quietened that voice, then made himself agree to his sister's suggestion.

Chapter 12

Isabella

"Shall we be going to the Michaelmas Fair this year?" asked her cousin Grace. The family had attended church service earlier this morning and were now back at Stanton Hall, taking their seats for luncheon. With Isabella were her brother Daniel, Ambrose Cranshaw and his sister, Sarah, as well as Grace and her husband, Benedict, with their young daughter, Anna.

Isabella played distractedly with the napkin on her lap, her thoughts far away. It had been three days since that last encounter with Silas Wilson, and of course, in those three days, she had not stopped going over every part of their conversation, from the spine tingling *"I'll be taking care of you just as soon as we're done with the work here"* to what he had said as they rode home, *"I may not be the gentleman you desire, but even I know the right thing is to see you home safely."*

What could he have meant by that last remark? Did he not see that the opposite was true? Of course, he was the one she desired. What could have made him think otherwise? Was it her refusal to have an affair with him? Surely he realised that she was not the sort of person to have love affairs with men. Then again, she had engaged in wanton intimacies with him that day in the carriage. Did he, after that, think of her as a hussy? Had she indelibly cheapened herself in his eyes? All these questions were tying her up in knots, taking up space in her mind night and day.

"Isabella! Did you hear what I said?" came Grace's voice again.

She looked up at her cousin then. "Pardon me, Gracie. What was it you said?"

"Were you wool-gathering, Bella?" enquired Grace. "One would think you had fallen in love."

"In love!" exclaimed Daniel. "I should like to know who with." He fixed his sister with his regard, brow knitted in concentration. "Is it Edwin Morton?"

"No, of course not," protested Isabella. "What nonsense this is. Do please stop this train of thought."

"Well then," retorted Grace, "what was on your mind just now that you did not listen to a word I said?"

Isabella shook her head. "Nothing of any import. Now tell me again, what was it you said."

"I asked if we were going to the Michaelmas Fair."

Isabella took a sip of her wine before replying, "I have no idea. Shall we go? We can if you like."

"We had great fun last year. I think we should," declared Grace.

"Are we all in agreement?" enquired Isabella of the others.

Daniel looked across at his estate manager and friend. "What think you, Ambrose?" he asked.

But it was Sarah that answered on her brother's behalf. "I think it is a splendid idea. Let us all go and make a group of it." She paused and went on, as if struck by a thought, "Perhaps we should invite Mr Templeton to join our party."

Isabella sighed inwardly. She well knew of Sarah's not so secret obsession with Philip Templeton, a handsome gentleman of some standing in the village. It was a hopeless obsession, for Mr Templeton had not shown the slightest interest in poor Sarah. Nevertheless, Isabella put on an agreeable smile as she replied, "What a good idea! Daniel, do write to Mr Templeton and invite him to join us at the fair."

So it was that the following week, a merry group set out from Stanton Hall to go to the Michaelmas Fair which was being held in a nearby town. They arrived at their destination just after midday and soon began exploring the various stalls and their wares. The fair was busy, and Daniel insisted she walk arm in arm with him, keeping a firm hold of her reticule in case of pickpockets. As they strolled through the crowds, Isabella searched with her eyes for any glimpse of Silas and his children, remembering how keen they had been to come to the fair. In vain did she look, but there was no sign of them in the busy thoroughfare.

They stopped to buy gingerbread at one stall, and various nick-nacks at another. Eventually, they reached the ballad-seller, who had a great many ballad sheets to sell for a penny each. On request, the ballad-seller was happy to pick up his concertina and sing the tune in question. "Oh please will you sing us this one," begged Grace holding a ballad sheet towards him. Obligingly, the man began to play and sing:

"What will you do, love, when I am going
With white sail flowing,
The seas beyond—
What will you do, love, when waves divide us,
And friends may chide us
For being fond?"
"Tho' waves divide us—and friends be chiding,
In faith abiding,
I'll still be true!
And I'll pray for thee on the stormy ocean,
In deep devotion—
That's what I'll do!"

He sang two further verses, and once he was done, was rewarded with much clapping of hands. "Very charming," drawled Mr Templeton, standing nearby, holding up another ballad sheet, "but I should now like to hear this one." And the ballad-seller once more picked up his concertina and began to sing another song. Thus they whiled away the time, picking through the ballad sheets and listening to various tunes.

It was during a lull between songs that Isabella heard her name being called. "Miss Stanton! Miss Stanton! Over here." She looked about and spotted Theodora Wilson waving excitedly at her. Beside Theodora was her younger brother, but Isabella's eyes were caught by the sight of the powerful figure standing immediately behind them—Silas. Isabella's heart began to pound rapidly in her chest as their two gazes collided. But then, she noticed something else and froze. A lady stood beside him, her arm tucked closely in his. The lady was pretty, with blond ringlets peeking below her becoming bonnet. At a glance, Isabella judged her to be around thirty, far closer to Silas in age than she was.

There was no further time to think as very soon, the Wilsons were upon them. "Miss Stanton, you were right about this fair," cried Theodora, her face wreathed in smiles.

The girl's high spirits helped break the tension that had begun to form in the air around Isabella. With a smile, she responded, "I take it you are enjoying yourself, Theo. I am glad of it. And what of Samuel?"

He stepped forward, proudly holding up the wind-up toy in his hands. "I found this," he said, showing it off. It was a small boat made of tin.

She took it from him and examined it carefully. "I am guessing you will soon want to test it on the water," she said with an arch look at him.

Samuel nodded eagerly. "Yes, I shall," he said. "Look, Miss Stanton. When I wind it up, the paddles start to turn."

Isabella observed the toy's mechanism with interest, then injected a stern note into her voice. "I hope you will remember to heed your father's words, Samuel, about never venturing out near the water without an adult."

"Oh, he will," replied Silas confidently.

Isabella's attention returned to Silas, who now addressed her with a greeting, "Good day, Miss Stanton."

"Good day, Mr Wilson," she replied. Remembering her manners, she made the introductions. "This is my brother, Daniel Stanton," she said, then went on to introduce the rest of the party, all the while conscious of the blonde lady still clinging to Silas's arm.

Daniel smiled warmly at him. "So, you are the new tenant at Netherwick Hall. I hope, sir, that you are comfortably settled there."

Silas inclined his head. "Indeed I am," he said. "And now it is my turn to make introductions. This is Mrs Corbett, a good family friend. And over here is my sister, Esther Driscoll, and her husband, Dr Driscoll, whom you may already know by reputation."

At this, Benedict, her cousin Grace's husband, spoke up, "Dr Driscoll, we meet again. I remember well the interesting discussion we had some years ago on the beneficial effects of chloroform."

"Ah, Mr Sedgwick, it is good to see you again. Well I remember our discussion…"

The conversation ebbed and flowed around her, but all Isabella was conscious of was Silas, and this good family friend who seemed welded to his side. Isabella pasted a smile to her face and tried to appear nonchalant, but inside she raged with fury and pain. It had not taken long for Silas to transfer his affections to another, so it seemed. Isabella could not help making comparisons between herself and the good lady. Ostensibly, Mrs Corbett seemed a far better match for Silas than Isabella could ever be. She was closer to him in age, a widow too it turned out, and she hailed from the same social class. It was also apparent that Silas was courting this lady, quite properly, everything above board. Isabella was racked with jealousy.

In that instant, her gaze met with his, and something of her pain must have shown, for she saw his eyes narrow and his lips flatten to a thin line. Was he feeling remorse for the shabby way he had treated her? Good, he should, though there was hollow satisfaction in the knowledge. All Isabella could think was that she had been deemed good enough for a salacious romp in a closed carriage but not to be courted openly as a prospective bride. Oh, the hurt! She ignored the fact that she herself had had misgivings about a marriage match with Silas and that she had been the one to reject his advances. Yes, on the surface they appeared mismatched, and the situation was not ideal. But had not Silas fought his way up in the world to make his fortune? Why then could he not fight equally hard to win her?

The answer to that question was unbearably simple. She did not matter enough. And with that realisation, Isabella knew she simply had to get away. She was about to open her mouth to say they should be heading back home, when she heard Silas issue an invitation to them. "I am holding a house party at Netherwick Hall this weekend," he said. "It would be a great honour if you could join us. There will be plenty of sport and good food."

To her horror, she heard Daniel agree. "Thank you, Mr Wilson. We shall look forward to it." Would Mrs Corbett be at this house party? Isabella felt quite sure she would be, and she had no desire to be a fly on the wall while Silas conducted his courtship of the pretty widow. It seemed though, she was to be given very little choice in the matter.

Chapter 13

Silas

Silas was growing tired of all this uncertainty. Isabella had rebuffed him, quite unequivocally. Yet here she was casting pained looks at him. He wished she would make up her mind good and proper. Did she want him or not? It really was not that difficult a question. He certainly knew his mind. He wanted her—had done so from the day they met.

All this shilly-shallying had to stop, he decided. It was giving him sleepless nights and occupying far too much of his daytime thoughts. Good Lord, he was even being made to feel like some sort of cad for having Mrs Corbett on his arm. In point of fact, that lady's hand was now beginning to feel like a hot coal that needed to be urgently cast off. Of course, good manners—which he did have—dictated that he should continue to escort her about the fair, when all he wanted was to drag Bella to the nearest private corner and have it out with her.

So, he came up with the next best thing. He invited Bella and her brother to his weekend house party. Surely during that time at his house, he could finally get to the bottom of this. And if then, it became absolutely clear that there was to be no future with Isabella, he would employ all his energy on ridding himself of his feelings for her, even if it meant moving to another part of the country. He did not like the idea of uprooting his children once more, but even less did he like the thought of continuing on this see-saw of feelings, going from hope to despair at the whim of Isabella Stanton. Really, there were times when he felt like putting that young lady across his knees and spanking her in punishment for all the aggravation she had caused him. Perhaps one day, he would—now that was a tantalising thought.

As he walked about the fair with Mrs Corbett on his arm, his mind formulated a plan. He had to get Isabella alone during that house party and have a forthright discussion of their situation. He would get straight to the point and put his cards on the table. With no ambiguity, he would tell her of his feelings and his wish to make her his wife. Though he might not be born to the nobility, he had wealth enough to ensure she lived in the highest comfort. If this was not good enough for Isabella and she refused him, then he would have his answer once and for all.

On the other hand, should she accept his proposal, then he would seek out her brother for a private interview and make arrangements for their nuptials forthwith. If he had anything to do with it, Isabella would be his wife before the year was out.

"It was very kind of you to include me in your house party, Mr Wilson," said Mrs Corbett in a gentle voice. "I can see I shall be in illustrious company with the addition of Viscount and Lady Isabella Stanton."

Lady Isabella Stanton. He had not realised that Isabella had a title, although of course, it made sense if her grandfather had been the Earl of Stanton. It was another reminder of the barrier in the way of their union—she was an aristocrat and he a mere commoner. He wondered why Isabella did not insist people use her title when being addressed. He was quite sure she had been introduced to him as Miss Stanton. Perhaps it was because such things as titles did not matter to her. On further reflection, he was sure of it. The Isabella who had toiled in the fields with him was not a snob, as she had been at pains to tell him.

He behoved himself to respond to Mrs Corbett. "Illustrious they may be in the eyes of the world, but they are just people like us all. I do hope you will not let that interfere with your enjoyment of the weekend."

"Oh, not at all. I do look forward to it," Mrs Corbett hastened to say.

Silas cast her a quick glance. Here was another problem to resolve. He could see quite clearly now that he could not, under any circumstance, propose marriage to Violet Corbett, excellent female though she might be. Not when his heart had set itself on someone else. Even should Isabella refuse him, he could not simply transfer his affections to another. It had been a mistake to encourage any hope in that direction. He could acknowledge now that in the fog of emotion that had beset him lately, he had failed to think clearly. But now his mind was clear, and so he would set things straight. Of course, he could not withdraw the invitation to his house party, but he would find a way to convey his change of heart as tactfully as possible. And there was no better time than now.

He cleared his throat. "I am hoping, Mrs Corbett, that there will be something for everyone to enjoy at the house party. I know Samuel is eager to welcome your son, John, and to show off his toys. I am sure he shall want to take his new boat out for a sail on the lake, though it will be under strict supervision, I assure you. As for Theodora, she shall have the pleasure of her cousins' company. I know it will do her good to be in the society of young girls her age."

"I am sure it will," enthused Mrs Corbett.

He paused, then went on, hoping she would read between the lines, "And we menfolk will no doubt enjoy a spot of shooting and perhaps fishing too, leaving you ladies to go for pleasurable strolls around the parkland and take tea on the terrace, which has wonderful views. I know my sister most particularly is looking forward to spending time with you, who have been such a good friend to her."

"Yes," murmured Mrs Corbett, "it will be good to spend time with Esther."

"As for the illustrious company, I am sure once you become better acquainted with Isabella, you will find her unaffected and quite lacking in any pretensions. She grew up in America, you see, where her family's title had little import."

Mrs Corbett glanced at him curiously. "You speak of the lady knowledgeably."

Silas smiled, thinking of Bella. "I am well acquainted with the lady and have a great admiration for her."

There was a long silence as Mrs Corbett digested this information. Perhaps he had lacked subtlety in his speech and could have let her down more gently, but subtlety was not one of his talents—truthfulness was. He hoped she would appreciate his straight talking.

She nodded her head. "In that case, I look forward to better acquainting myself with Lady Isabella. Esther too will want to further her acquaintance with the good lady."

"Bella can be quite fiery and argumentative, but she is loyal to a fault and the bravest female I have ever met," continued Silas. Now that the floodgates had opened, it seemed he could not stop rhapsodising about her.

"You must love her very much," said Mrs Corbett softly.

"Madly." He snorted. "I am sorry, Mrs Corbett. I had not meant to unburden myself so."

She laughed. "That is quite alright, Mr Wilson. I am glad to know the truth of the matter, and I wish you luck with the lady."

"Thank you. I can quite see, Mrs Corbett, why you are such a good friend of Esther's."

They had by now reached his sister's carriage. He handed Mrs Corbett up into it and bid everyone farewell, then went on to his own carriage, where the children and Miss Grainger were already ensconced. Over the course of the journey home, he listened absently to his children's chatter, but his mind was elsewhere. In two days' time, Isabella would be coming to Netherwick Hall, and he would get one last chance to win her over.

Chapter 14

Isabella

Isabella and Daniel set out for Netherwick Hall in their carriage early on Saturday morning. They would spend the day and the night there, then return the following morning. As the horses' hooves clip clopped over the paved road, Isabella stared unseeingly out of the window, excitement and anticipation swirling in equal measure within her breast.

The thought of seeing Silas again fired up the blood in her veins. For weeks now, he had dominated her thoughts, night and day. She was drawn to him like a bee to honey. She wanted to see him again so very much, yet she did not care to witness him wooing another lady. The jealousy that had ignited on seeing him with Mrs Corbett at the Michaelmas Fair had continued to rage unabated. How dare he switch his attentions to someone else?

Along with the jealousy came a strong streak of possessiveness. Silas was meant for her. She was sure of it. Two people did not kiss the way they had kissed without it meaning something. And had he not said it was the best kiss he had ever had? She had been foolish to put up so many impediments to their marriage in her head. Now, she reasoned with herself. Silas may have loved his wife, but he gave every appearance to be ready to marry again. It was true he was a dozen years older, yet he was still in his prime and full of vitality. And as for the gap in their social status, what did it matter in the grand scheme of things? People would talk, that was true. Was she going to let something as silly as gossip stand in the way of her happiness?

Then came more sobering thoughts. Maybe she was wrong about everything, just as she had been wrong about Silas's character. Maybe he did not have feelings for her other than a passing physical attraction. Maybe she had foolishly built all this up in her mind to be far more than it actually was.

Oh, what she would give to stop being so confused!

Her perturbation did not go unnoticed by the other occupant in the carriage. "What is the matter with you, Bella?" asked her brother. "Are you ailing?"

"I do not know what you can mean," she retorted.

"Yes, you do. You have not been your usual self lately. And just now, you were biting your lips and making a most distressed looking face. Out with it, Bella."

"I… it is nothing," she mumbled.

He frowned, clearly disbelieving. She looked away, blinking her eyes, for she realised there were unwelcome tears gathering in them.

"What is it?" asked Daniel softly. "You know you can tell me."

Isabella sniffed. Could she tell her brother? She took a shaky breath and began, "Have you ever had strong feelings for someone who, to all appearances, was absolutely wrong for you?"

A shadow crossed Daniel's face. "Yes, Bella," he said to her. "I have." He considered her words then, reaching the correct conclusion. Her brother always was too clever for his boots. "Silas Wilson," he stated matter-of-factly.

Isabella did not disabuse him of the notion. Daniel was quiet a moment, then mused out loud, "He is quite a few years older than you."

"That does not signify," she replied crossly.

Daniel laughed. "No, I suppose not, if you love him. But Bella, you have not known him long. Are you sure of your feelings?"

Isabella nodded quickly. "I believe so."

Daniel, however, was not convinced. "When I was your age, Bella, I thought myself in love with a certain young lady of my acquaintance and was all set to propose. Papa, though, advised me to wait and test my true sentiments over a period of time. He was right you know, for my passion waned, and I was not even a little heartbroken when the lady accepted a marriage proposal from someone else."

"I may not have time," said Isabella shakily, "for he is all set to court another lady already."

"If he is so fickle as to do so, then he cannot be right for you."

"I think it may be partly my fault," said Isabella in a small voice. "I may have… well, I may have rebuffed his advances."

Daniel sighed in exasperation. "Now why would you do such a thing? No, don't tell me. I can already surmise. You took up against him because he made his fortune from cotton mills. I well remember your feelings on the matter the day you went to show him around Netherwick Hall."

Isabella cringed at the memory. It was true that she had voiced doubts as to the merits of renting her home to someone in trade and her fear that Mr Wilson would prove to be "vulgar and uncouth." But she had not truly meant those words. They were only a mask for those other feelings she had regarding the Confederacy, against which her brother Benjamin was daily risking his life. In her mind, she had conflated all mill owners with that enemy, but she had been wrong to do so. What she had seen of Silas—the way he had helped the Shaws, the generous manner he treated his household staff who sang his praises, even the care he had taken to look out for her wellbeing after her mishap in the water—all these things spoke volumes of his morals. He was a good person, and she had turned her nose up at him.

"I did beg his forgiveness for the things I said," she whispered, "but then I told him marriage was out of the question."

"Oh, Bella."

"I was trying to protect my feelings, for I did not think he wished to marry me, only to dally with me."

"And what, pray tell, put this notion into your head?" asked Daniel, his tone severe.

"You are my brother," said Isabella primly. "These are not things I can speak of with you."

"What things?" demanded Daniel.

Isabella was not going to elucidate, so she merely maintained a haughty silence.

Daniel narrowed his eyes at her. "Isabella, please tell me that this man has not taken your virtue."

"I—well, strictly speaking, no."

Daniel growled dangerously, "I have no wish to know what you meant by that vague response, but listen here. No matter what may have occurred between you and Silas Wilson, I want your word, Bella, that from here on you will not engage in any unbecoming behaviour. If he has feelings for you, then let him court you the honourable way. Your word, Bella."

"Oh," she sputtered, "very well."

"You will make sure never to be alone in his company," continued Daniel sternly.

This threw her plans into disarray, for of course, she had thought to seek Silas out for private discourse. "But how else are we to talk things out?" she asked plaintively.

"Nonsense! You are perfectly able to talk to him without anyone overhearing you, only make sure you are always within sight of others. Your word on that too, Bella."

Isabella observed him in annoyance. "Alright, but only for the duration of this house party. You are a very tiresome brother sometimes," she said irritably.

He grinned. "I will take that as a compliment. Now stop with the long face, Bella. I have nothing against Mr Wilson, and Ambrose had only good things to say about him when I made my enquiries. So cheer up! You are about to spend a whole day at his house, and I am sure there shall be plenty of opportunity for you to 'talk things out'."

Just then, their carriage drew up outside the front entrance of Netherwick Hall. Glancing through the window, Isabella spied Silas standing at the top of the steps, watching their arrival. Her heart skipped several beats. This was it, her chance to finally make things right with Silas Wilson. She vowed she would not let it slip through her fingers.

Chapter 15

Silas

Silas did not have much experience in the hosting of weekend house parties. He had never had time for such frivolities in his old life in Manchester, for he had been far too busy managing his manufacturing empire. Although this would be a small party by the standards of the day, he still wished to ensure all was proper, especially as Isabella would be one of his guests.

He spoke to his groundskeeper to ensure there were plenty of pheasants to be had for hunting. Croquet would be laid out on the lawn for their entertainment, and guests could also play a game of billiards in the sun room if they so wished. Added to which, of course, there would be a generous amount of good food. Once more, he had adjured Mrs Jones to do him proud with the many meals that would be offered—breakfast, a picnic lunch, afternoon tea and then an elaborate dinner. For the evening, card games were planned followed perhaps by a game of charades. None of these activities were to Silas's taste, but since this party had been foisted upon him, he would do it and do it right.

His sister and her family, along with Mrs Corbett and her son, had arrived earlier this morning and were now sitting down to breakfast. Silas had little appetite for food, contenting himself with a few slices of cold beef and a small bread roll, while his guests partook of the extensive array of dishes laid out on the sideboard. He nibbled absently on his roll and took a sip of his coffee, his feet drumming impatiently under the table. When would they get here?

Presently, a footman came in and spoke quietly in his ear. A carriage had been seen turning into the driveway that led to the house. At once, Silas rose to his feet and made his excuses. With quick strides he went to the front entrance of the house and watched Isabella arrive. He saw her glance out of the carriage window and catch sight of him. Their gazes remained upon each other as he hurried down the front steps and waited for the carriage to come to a stop. Viscount Stanton jumped down first, before assisting his sister out of the vehicle.

Isabella's brother greeted him with a jovial smile. "Good day, Mr Wilson. I hope we are not arrived too late."

"Only a little," replied Silas in all seriousness.

He then turned his attention to Isabella, ignoring the viscount's amusement, and bowed. "Bella, it is good to see you," he spoke gruffly.

He saw the colour rise to her cheeks as she replied, her voice not quite steady, "It is good to be here, Mr Wilson." *Silas*, he whispered to her in his head. *Call me Silas.*

For a long moment, he stood gazing down at her, not missing the rapid rise and fall of her chest as she took each breath. Their rapt interlude was interrupted by the clearing of a throat and the viscount saying, "Well, I suppose we had better go inside."

Reminded of his duties as host, Silas stepped back and ushered his guests into the house. Their travel cases were unloaded and brought in, and a servant showed them to their rooms. Silas had Isabella stay in the pink damask room that she had used the previous time. It was the prettiest of the guest rooms, occupying a spacious corner of the house and affording picturesque views of the gardens. It also had the advantage of being positioned next to Silas's own bedchamber at the end of the corridor, with no other room nearby.

Silas had instructed his household staff to prepare the bed with fresh linen, made of the finest Egyptian cotton from his factories, and to place a vase of freshly cut flowers on the mantelpiece. He'd also requested they put a platter with an assortment of fruits in the room for Bella's delectation. On the bedside table, Silas had himself carefully placed a copy of Charlotte Brontë's Villette and Jane Austen's Persuasion, two of her favourite books.

He had racked his brain thinking of ways to make her as comfortable as possible during her stay at Netherwick Hall. Jars of fragrant lotions and perfumes lined the dressing table, next to a newly purchased silver and enamel hairbrush. A large bath tub had been carried into the room and put by the fireplace, with maids at the ready to fill it with steaming hot water whenever Bella required it. Laid on a chair beside the tub were the softest of towels—also made in his factories. On a nearby table, he had left a handwritten note for Bella, set beside a dish of soap infused with the essence of orange blossoms. He had detected hints of that scent whenever he was near Bella, and it had soon become his favourite aroma. He had even instructed his servants to scent the pillows on his bed with it so he could breathe it in at night.

As he returned to the dining room to await Isabella and her brother there, he hoped the room was to her liking. He had turned into a lovesick fool, he knew, yet he was unable to stop himself from wanting to ensure everything was perfect for Bella. Perhaps indirectly, he wished to convey the message: "Be mine, and you shall live like a queen." In business, he had never been one to take half measures when he determined on a course of action, and when it came to love, it seemed he was equally thorough. He was going all out to win Isabella Stanton, for he could not let her slip through his fingers.

Chapter 16

Isabella

Isabella entered the pink damask room and breathed in the scent of fresh flowers. Looking around, she perceived a luscious bouquet had been placed in a vase over the mantelpiece. She went to it and ran a finger along the softness of a petal, trying to calm the furious pounding of her heart.

Once she had achieved a degree of equanimity, she took an exploratory walk around the room, noting the profusion of scented jars on the dressing table, a large bathing tub and next to it, a handwritten note signed by Silas:

Bella,

Ring the bell for hot water at any hour whenever you wish to have the bath filled. I have asked for fruit to be left in your room, but should you wish for any other refreshment, please also do not hesitate to ask. Your comfort is paramount.

Yours,

Silas

Isabella stroked a finger over his signed name, a half-smile hovering on her mouth. Finally, she put the note down and continued her tour of the room. She stopped by the tub and stroked a hand over the soft towel, then picked up the soap dish, breathing in the aroma of orange blossoms. How had he known it was her favourite scent? Her perambulation ended at the well-sprung bed covered in the softest of sheets. She sat on the edge of it and leaned over to the side table, taking hold of the top book. It was Jane Austen's Persuasion. She remembered mentioning over luncheon, the last time she had been here, that this was one of her favourite novels along with—she reached out for the other book, and yes, it was Villette. Silas had remembered, and he had been thoughtful enough to procure a copy of each book for her.

What could this all mean? Her heart gave a joyful response, but her mind urged caution. It would be foolhardy to jump to conclusions. After a moment, she rose to her feet again. The rest of the party was sitting down to breakfast and waiting for her to join them. Quickly, she availed herself of the commode in the dressing room, washed her face and hands, brushed out her hair with the fancy silver and enamel brush, and pinned it up neatly. Then, she went down to the dining room.

She entered it to the sound of laughter and convivial conversation. Immediately, Silas rose to his feet and beckoned her. "Bella, come sit over here," he said in that commanding voice she loved.

She went over to sit at the table beside him. The hum of conversation had died down and all eyes were upon her. The party gathered could not have failed to notice Silas addressing her by the shortened version of her given name, a familiarity only usually allowed between family and close friends. She looked up to see her brother raise an amused brow. Silas's sister, on the other hand, did not look amused in the slightest. In point of fact, she was shooting daggers with her eyes at Silas.

He ignored them all and turned to Isabella, examining her face with that fierce gaze she had come to associate with him. "Will you have tea or coffee, Bella?" he asked in a low rumble.

"Coffee, please."

He poured her a cup, then added a dash of milk. "Sugar?"

"One lump, please."

He dropped it into her coffee and stirred it before handing the cup to her. She was conscious of everyone's eyes on them as he executed this solicitous task. Silas was the only one, it seemed, uncaring of the attention. His gaze was on her once more. "What will you have to eat, Bella?" he enquired. "Are you hungry?"

"I—I..." she felt unable to speak.

"She ought to be," answered Daniel on her behalf, "as she has not eaten a single bite today."

"In that case," said Silas, "let me make up a plate for you." He stood and went to the sideboard, loading up a plate with eggs, meats, slices of cheese and some freshly baked bread rolls. While he did so, Isabella stared down at the tablecloth, overcome with shyness and something else—a soaring light-headedness. Perhaps it was due to being hungry. Or perhaps it had everything to do with Silas.

He came back presently with a generously filled plate and placed it before her. "Eat," he barked out, without regard for social niceties. And obediently, she ate. She felt him stand and go to the sideboard once more, this time returning with a plate for himself. It seemed he too was hungry.

Slowly, conversation around them resumed. The day's activities were discussed. As soon as breakfast was over, the men would head to the woods for some pheasant shooting, promising to bag a good many birds for their game pie that evening. The ladies would have a leisurely morning, reading on the terrace or strolling in the gardens, after which they would all convene on the lawn for a picnic lunch.

Isabella basked under the power of Silas's attention. It was as if only the two of them were at the dining table. He spoke quietly to her as they ate. "What shall you do this morning?" he wanted to know.

"I suppose I will read on the terrace," she murmured. "Thank you for the books you left for me. I am surprised you remembered."

"I have not forgotten a thing, Bella," he said on a low growl. "Which book will you read today?"

Isabella pondered for a moment then said, "I believe I shall read Persuasion."

"What is it about this work that pleases you so?" he wondered, adding, "I have read it recently myself and enjoyed it, but I am curious to know your thoughts."

Isabella set down her fork. "Well," she said, "as with all works by Jane Austen, it is brilliantly observed and written with great wit, but I suppose what I like most about it is that it is about second chances." Her voice tailed off to a low mumble, "We all make mistakes after all."

She felt Silas's sharp intake of breath at her words. "And when we do make mistakes," he completed her sentence, "it behoves us to do everything in our power to correct them."

"Yes," she said, not daring to look into his eyes.

"Then that is what we shall do, my love," he said, only for her ears.

Isabella felt her spirits soar. There was no longer any doubting his intent. This was confirmed a moment later as Silas spoke again, very quietly, seemingly wanting to ensure there was no mistaking his purpose. "And know this, Bella. It is not to be a tawdry affair, but that other thing that involves a ring."

Isabella nodded, feeling as if her heart would burst with happiness. On the wave of that happiness came something else—a tingling of her nerve endings and a now familiar ache at the core of her body. She may have been surrounded by people, but her body did not seem to care. It wanted Silas and his touch. It wanted to reach that pinnacle of pleasurable sensation. On the mere whisp of a breath, she murmured his name, "Silas."

She did not know how, but he knew and understood at once. He leaned forward to whisper in her ear, "Patience, my love. I'll be taking care of you just as soon as I get you to myself."

She could not but be aware that her room was immediately next to his bedchamber in a deserted part of the corridor. Her heart beat double-time at the thought of his paying her a visit this night. But then, she remembered something else. "We cannot," she whispered back.

"Whyever not?" he hissed, a scowl returning to his face.

"Daniel made me promise I would never be alone in your company."

"The hell he did!" Silas whispered back on an angry hiss, finding her brother with his eyes and glowering in his direction. It seemed Daniel too understood the purport of the conversation, for he merely responded with a smug smile on his countenance.

After a moment's reflection, Silas spoke again, so low that only she could hear. "In that case, my love, you will have to take matters into your own hands, just this time. I want you to go up to your bedchamber now and lock the door. Then I want you to remove every stitch of your clothing and lie under the sheet in your bed, feeling the soft kiss of the fine cotton on your naked skin. I want you to close your eyes and touch your body with your hands, imagining it is me touching you."

She breathed quickly, in short, sharp bursts, thinking about the decadent thing she was about to do. But Silas was not finished. Leaning close, he whispered into her ear, "Fill your hands with your luscious breasts the way I long to do. Then pinch the tips with your fingers—make it sting, just a little. Imagine the sting is my teeth taking a tug of you."

Isabella trembled. She cast quick, nervous glances around the table. Daniel was watching them intently. So too was Esther

Driscoll, Silas's sister. But surely neither of them could guess what was being said.

Silas continued in a hoarse whisper, "Then I want your hand to move down, all the way to your womanly mound. Touch yourself there, my love. Use two fingers, wet them in your juices and swirl them delicately over your pleasure nub, like I did before. Only this time, imagine it is my tongue there, not my fingers. Stroke yourself over and over, and do not stop until you pulsate with your orgasm. Go now and do what I asked. I shall be thinking of you as you do it."

Abruptly, Silas stood. "I believe, gentlemen, it is time for us to do some hunting," he said gruffly. "Ladies, do excuse us. We shall meet with you again at luncheon." His eyes drilled into hers, clearly expecting that she follow his instructions.

She rose hastily and mumbled an excuse, then rushed out of the dining room and up the stairs. Once in her room, she locked the door and leaned against it for a moment, regaining her breath. An instant later, she was tugging loose the fastenings of her dress and pulling it over her head. Her shoes came off next, then her corset and all her undergarments until she stood, bare and shivering.

Next, she was on the bed, getting under the covers and feeling the sensual brush of the fine cotton sheets on her naked skin. Her body quivered in fevered excitement. Remembering Silas's instructions, she brought her hands to her full breasts, cupping them with a gentle squeeze. Eyes closed, she imagined it was Silas fondling her. A moan escaped her lips.

Then she tugged each nipple between her thumb and forefinger, envisioning Silas's mouth there. Oh, what a tantalising picture that was! She pinched her nipples again, feeling a corresponding throb between her thighs. Writhing sensuously under the sheet, she slipped one hand downward, keeping the other at her tingling breast. Her fingers encountered the soft curls of her mound then moved further down to the moist flesh hidden beneath. She dipped two digits into her wet core, before finding the small nub of flesh at the apex of her thighs and beginning to draw circles over it. Another moan slipped through her lips.

How good it felt to touch herself there! Why had she never known to do this before? On and on she stroked, feeling her pleasure grow. But much as she savoured the touch of her fingers, she knew that Silas's touch was infinitely better. He had spoken of stroking her with his tongue. What would it feel like to have him lap delicately at her flesh? The answering clench of her core told her it would be delightful.

She continued to stroke herself, fast and frantically, imagining Silas with his face buried between her legs, his tongue eagerly licking her in that intimate place. "Ah," she sighed, panting with the exertion, but did not let up the furious stroking of her fingers. She could feel her pleasure build with each stroke. "Oh," she moaned, very nearly at the pinnacle. And when her body began to pulsate with the bliss of her release, she let out a loud, heedless cry. Then, she lay back on the bed, spent, drifting into a contented reverie.

Eventually, she exerted herself to rise, wash off the sticky residue of her pleasure and get dressed. Once she was presentable again, she went down to the terrace, taking her book along with her. There, she found Esther Driscoll and Violet Corbett lounging languidly on deck chairs. They greeted her in polite tones as she settled on a nearby chair. A servant quickly came over to offer tea and a tray of delectable cakes. Goodness, more food! However, her activities in the bedroom had left her hungry again, and she accepted a small slice of Victoria Sponge.

"We are fortunate with the weather today, Lady Isabella," began Mrs Corbett graciously. "It is pleasantly warm and dry for this time of the year. One could almost believe we are still in summer."

"Yes," replied Isabella. "I am sure when Silas issued the invitations for this house party, he commanded the gods to bring us good weather, and they naturally heeded his instructions."

Mrs Corbett laughed delightedly. "I can quite imagine it. Mr Wilson strikes me as the sort of person whom no one wishes to displease, least of all the gods."

"Lady Isabella," interjected Mrs Driscoll crisply. "You seem to be on remarkably familiar terms with my brother. I do wish you would enlighten me as to how that came to be."

Isabella set down her cup, refusing to be discomposed by this inquisition. She had not been mistress of her own affairs these past two years without learning how to stand up for herself. "I believe, Mrs Driscoll," she replied calmly, "that it would be best to address such enquiries to Silas, for I certainly cannot, upon such short acquaintance as mine is with you, discuss matters of a personal nature. Now, if you will excuse me, I will go look in on Theodora and Samuel."

She rose majestically to her feet, her book in hand, nodded a dismissal and walked briskly away. As she passed by Mrs Corbett, she thought she saw a fleeting expression of amusement cross her face. Mrs Driscoll, by contrast, appeared to be thunderstruck that someone so young should speak to her so. Isabella gave a mental shrug. There were matters of far greater import happening in her life at this time than to be worrying about what Silas's sister or Mrs Corbett thought of her. If, as she hoped, she was to become Silas's wife, there would be time enough to mend bridges with his sister.

His children, however, were another matter. It occurred to her, perhaps for the first time, that quite possibly soon, she would be a mother to them. The thought did not fill her with too great a degree of anxiety, for she was already on easy terms with them and liked them enormously. Still, it would not hurt to strengthen the bonds of their existing relationship. With this in mind, she enquired from a nearby footman as to the location of the children, and learning that they were out on the lawn playing croquet, she hastened to join them.

She found them in the middle of a game with their two cousins, who looked to be a year or two older than Theodora. Isabella went up to them with a smile. As soon as he caught sight of her, Samuel gave an exaggerated sigh. "Oh good," he cried. "Miss Stanton can take over from me." So saying, he handed her the mallet. "This game is quite boring," he declared as she took it from him.

"Only because you're no good at it," accused Theodora.

One of her cousins, the one who seemed the eldest, gave Samuel a very reproving look and chided, "Samuel, you are remiss with your manners. You should not be addressing the lady as Miss Stanton but as Lady Isabella Stanton."

Samuel shrugged, unconcerned. "I've always called her Miss Stanton," he declared, "and she doesn't mind, do you?"

Isabella drew the boy into the crook of her arm. "I do not mind at all," she said smilingly at him. "In fact, Samuel, you could go one better and drop the formality altogether. How about you call me Bella from now on?"

The boy grinned delightedly, glad to have been given the upper hand when it came to his lecturing cousin. "Bella it is!" he crowed. "Now, I am going to find John and see if we can finally take my boat for a turn out on the lake."

Isabella stayed him with a hand on his arm. "You will not go there without Miss Grainger," she admonished.

"I know. I know," retorted Samuel. With that, he hurried away.

Isabella returned her attention to the group of girls. "Well now," she said. "How about a game of croquet?"

For the next hour they played in teams, with Isabella and Theodora on one side, and the two cousins, Estella and Marianne, on the other. It took a while for Isabella to notice, but she gradually became aware that Theodora seemed less ebullient than her usual self. At first, Isabella put it down to a natural shyness at having to entertain unfamiliar cousins. Soon, however, it occurred to her that something else was amiss.

When the game ended, Estella and Marianne suggested they all reconvene on the terrace for some refreshment. "What a good idea," enthused Isabella. "Why don't the two of you run up ahead, and I shall join you shortly." Turning to the young girl at her side, she added, "Theo, will you come up with me? There is something I need your help with."

"Of course," replied Theodora.

Together, they walked back to the house and up the stairs to the pink damask room. "What is it you wished me to help you with?" asked Theodora.

"I am unsure what I should wear for dinner tonight, as I brought two evening gowns with me," said Isabella, going to the wooden armoire and opening it to bring out the two dresses. "Will you help me decide what to wear?"

Theodora nodded shyly.

With a smile, Isabella laid out the dresses on the bed. "What do you think?" she asked the young girl.

Theodora ran her hands over the fabric of each gown, exclaiming, "They are both so pretty!"

"They are, aren't they?" concurred Isabella. The first gown was made of white silk with pink ruffles, flaring out in three separate layers of skirt. The other dress was in the palest blue silk, simpler in design but elegant, with an off-the-shoulder bodice trimmed with a delicate detail of pink lace flowers. "So, which shall it be?"

Theodora pursed her lips in concentration. "Maybe you should try them on first," she suggested.

"A good idea," agreed Isabella. For the second time that day, she undid the fastenings of her dress and took it off. "Which shall I try on first?" she asked.

"The white one," decided Theodora.

Isabella dutifully pulled on the white dress and patted the bodice down over her corseted waist. She twirled in front of Theodora and asked, "What do you think?"

"You look like a princess," declared the young girl.

Isabella chuckled. "I shall take that as a compliment. Well now, let me try on the other gown for you." With that, she took off the white dress and tried on the pale blue silk. "Now, what do you think?" she asked, posing in front of Theodora.

The young girl looked thoughtful. "It is very pretty, but I think I prefer the first dress."

"Very well," smiled Isabella. "The white gown it is, and thank you for helping me to decide." She did not immediately go to change dress again, instead going to sit on the edge of the bed and patting the space beside her. "Will you come sit here, Theo, and tell me what is bothering you?" she asked gently.

Theodora went to sit beside her but said, "There is nothing bothering me, Bella."

"I see. Well, let us imagine there was something on your mind. You know, it is always helpful to speak of it to someone, though not to anyone. It must be to someone who you can trust."

The young girl nodded.

"I haven't known you and Samuel very long," went on Isabella, "but I hope you can feel easy talking to me. I promise to listen with the greatest of sympathy and to try my best to help."

For a long while, the girl said nothing. Isabella did not wish to press her and was about to concede defeat when Theodora blurted out, "It's Estella."

"What about her?" asked Isabella quietly.

"She said—" Theodora began but could not go on.

"What did she say?" prompted Isabella.

In a low voice, Theodora continued, "She said the only reason we are rich is because Papa took advantage of poor workers in his factories, paying them a pittance and making them work all hours of the day. And she said Papa sold the factories and moved us here because his workers had finally had enough and gone on strike."

Isabella paled. This was much too close to some of the accusations she herself had hurled at Silas. Looking at the hurt on Theodora's face, she felt a wave of guilt once more for the way she had behaved, jumping to unfair conclusions.

She took a deep breath and gathered herself, trying to formulate an appropriate response. Gently, she asked, "And do you believe what Estella said?"

The girl look helplessly up at Isabella. "I do not know," she said in confusion.

"Well," said Isabella, "think about the sort of person you know your papa to be. Do you think this is something he would do, treat people unfairly just to make himself rich?"

Theodora shook her head adamantly. "No," she said.

"Then perhaps it is Estella who is mistaken."

The young girl sniffed. "But what if she isn't?"

"I think your papa is the best person to answer that, don't you?"

"He will get cross if I tell him," said Theodora in a small voice.

"Yes, I rather suspect he will, but not with you."

Theodora looked up at her. "Do you think I should tell him?"

Isabella sighed. "I think perhaps it would be best if you wait until the guests have left before you speak to him, but yes, this is something you should discuss with your papa. He will know the truth better than anyone else and can explain it all to you."

"Will you be there when I tell him? He is less likely to get cross if you are around."

Isabella frowned. "Why do you think that?"

Now Theodora hung her head shyly. "I think Papa likes you. When you are here, he smiles."

"Really? I am more used to seeing him looking very fierce."

Theodora gave a tinkling laugh. "Yes, he does that too, but in between, when you are there, he smiles."

Isabella drew the young girl into a quick embrace and dropped a kiss to the top of her head. "I will let you in on a secret, Theo."

"What is it?" Theodora asked, looking intrigued.

"I like your papa very much, and I do not believe a word of what Estella told you."

"Neither do I," replied Theodora staunchly.

"And if you wish me to be there when you speak to him about this, then I will, but let us wait until after this house party."

"Very well," agreed Theodora.

Isabella got to her feet. "Run along now, Theo, and join everyone on the terrace. I will get changed and come directly."

Once the girl had gone, Isabella sat down once more and took a moment to compose herself. She had no experience of motherhood, but she hoped she had acquitted herself reasonably well just now. The hurt look on Theodora's face had pulled at her heartstrings. Those remarks by Estella had been ungenerous and, she was sure, motivated by envy. Isabella did not know much about motherhood, but she knew very well the malice of young girls when bitten by the bug of jealousy. Her own envy of Silas's dead wife had caused her to say words, that day in the carriage, which she regretted deeply. In truth, she was no better than Estella, but this weekend house party was all about making things right again, and she was determined to do so.

She stood and quickly changed back into her morning dress, putting the two evening gowns away again in the armoire. Then, with a spring in her step as it was very nearly time for luncheon where she would see Silas again, she made her way down to the terrace once more.

Chapter 17

Silas

The men, equipped with their shotguns, walked towards the woods, the hounds at their heels. Silas had resigned himself to a dull morning engaged in what he considered a feckless sport—he would much rather be engaged in something far more pleasurable. The shooting of game was well and good in his view if one required to put meat on the table, but to do it for sport seemed pointless and cruel.

He had made arrangements though for all the pheasants shot today to be distributed to the poorer families in the village, as well as to the farming tenants hereabouts, with the exception of Mr Flint, whom he had no wish to reward in any way. That man in all probability did not know that in badmouthing Isabella, he had put himself on the wrong side of Silas. He would find it out soon enough.

To top it all, Silas was having to keep company with Isabella's brother Daniel, towards whom he was not feeling well disposed at all. On they walked, Daniel and Silas side by side, with Dr Driscoll and servants trailing behind them at a slower pace.

"It looks to be a fine day for a spot of hunting," remarked Daniel casually.

"Hmm," grunted Silas.

"I believe it is customary at weekend house parties of the ton to make wagers as to how many birds will be bagged," continued Daniel, undeterred.

"Thankfully, I am not a member of the ton," replied Silas.

"Nevertheless, I should be willing to place a wager on my prowess with the shotgun today. How about you, Mr Wilson?"

"I make it a point, sir, never to bet on anything unless I am sure of the outcome," bit back Silas.

"So, you will not join me in a wager?" enquired Daniel.

"No, but if you wish to place a wager on yourself, do feel free to do so. I shall be happy to take the funds off you when you lose."

Daniel burst into laughter. "What makes you so sure I will lose?"

"I am not so sure, hence why I will not place a bet myself," retorted Silas.

"Point taken." Daniel considered the matter then made his decision. "I shall wager you a guinea that I will bag two dozen birds or more today. If I lose, you may take the guinea off me, but if I win, I ask for one small thing."

Silas raised a brow. "What small thing would that be?"

Daniel's tone hardened. "I ask that you resolve matters with Bella so as to leave her with no uncertainty as to where she stands."

Silas gave a startled bark of laughter. "That is something I fully intend to do, with or without your wager."

"Nevertheless, I will let the wager stand, for I fully intend to win it. Please ensure, sir, that she is released from the purgatory of doubt," said Daniel coldly.

Silas could only snarl, "Then perhaps, sir, you will release her from the promise you made her make."

"What? Her promise to maintain her virtue? There is not a snowflake's chance in hell that I will release her from that!"

Silas paused a moment, disconcerted, but continued to make his point, "I meant, sir, her promise never to be alone in my company. I would prefer not to have an audience when I propose marriage."

"I am sorry to disappoint," chuckled Daniel, "but no, I do not propose to release her from that particular promise either, at least not until she is safely wed." On Silas's murderous stare, he amended that last point. "Or until she is betrothed and the banns read out."

Not to be outdone, Silas gritted out, "I can have the banns read out tomorrow at church, if that is to be the case."

"She hasn't accepted your proposal yet," reminded Daniel coolly.

"I am well aware!" growled Silas, nearing the end of his patience.

They had by now reached the edge of the woodland where they planned to hunt. Daniel stopped to face him. "Good," he said. "I think we understand each other. And now, time to hunt some birds."

Some two hours later, the final count of birds bagged by Daniel was in—twenty-eight. The dratted man even had the audacity to say with a smirk, "I too never bet on anything unless I am sure of the outcome."

Silas's tally was far lower at eleven, but there again, his mind had not been fully engaged on the task. No, he'd had far more pressing matters to think about, such as whether or not Bella would agree to marry him and how he would go about proposing without the privacy of being alone with her. And of course, his mind was also engaged in wondering if she had followed his instructions to touch herself. He was sure she had. He imagined her naked under the sheets, her fingers stroking her pleasure nub until she pulsed with her release. At this, he'd had to adjust his trousers, which had become uncomfortably tight around his groin.

Now, they headed back to the house for their luncheon. His thoughts had gone round and round in circles considering the matter of his proposal. He had decided, as ever, that there was no time like the present. This morning at breakfast, Bella had nodded when he had mentioned a ring, so he hoped he was not about to make an abject fool of himself. No matter if he did. He had made a promise to himself that he would put his cards on the table, and that was what he would do. It was a pity that he would have to contend with an audience while doing so, but he would not let that deter him.

Once at the house, he went quickly up to his bedchamber and refreshed his appearance. From a drawer in his bedside cabinet, he withdrew the small box that contained the ring he had purchased yesterday on his trip to the jeweller in Oxford. It featured a cluster of small diamonds around a larger stone in the centre. He had seen it and thought it would look just right on Bella's elegant hand. If she did not like it, however, they could always exchange it for something she preferred.

He sat on the edge of his bed, the box propped open in his palm to reveal the ring. For long moments, he pondered what to do. Then he stood, pocketing the ring, and left the room.

Chapter 18

Isabella

A large rug had been laid out on the lawn, and on it, a profusion of laden dishes. It should not have surprised Isabella, having experienced Silas's hospitality, that this picnic luncheon was to be a generous feast. There were meat pies and a large variety of delicately cut sandwiches. To one side was a long tray filled with berries, peaches and sliced pears. Cold chicken and finely sliced ham were to be found on another set of dishes, interspersed with platters of freshly baked bread from which drifted a delightful aroma.

Isabella took a seat on a cushion while servants scurried to set cutlery and plate before her, then to offer her a glass of cool lemonade. She looked about for Silas, but he was nowhere to be seen. Swallowing her disappointment, she helped herself to a slice of pear and munched on it, half listening to the chitchat around her. At last, she sensed his presence and turned her head quickly to see him marching towards them, a look of intense focus on his face. As ever, her heart picked up its pace at the sight of him.

He came to where she sat and leaned down to whisper something in Theodora's ear. His daughter nodded with a smile and rose rapidly to her feet, moving to sit a little further along the picnic rug. Silas dropped down onto the vacated cushion by Isabella's side. "Bella," he said, settling himself down. "Did you have a pleasing morning?"

She felt her cheeks flush at the implied meaning of his question. "Yes, Silas," she replied. "It was… very pleasing."

"Good." His deep voice was filled with satisfaction.

"More pleasing than Mr Wilson's morning was, I'm sure," interjected Daniel, who sat opposite them. "He only managed to bag a measly eleven pheasants and lost a wager to me in the bargain."

He exchanged a meaningful look with Silas who merely raised a brow in response and said, "Which I shall be honouring in due course."

"What sort of a wager," enquired Isabella.

Silas gave a brusque laugh. "You will find out soon enough, Bella." He offered her a bread roll and slid the butter dish in her direction.

As she buttered her roll, a footman approached with a letter on a salver. "A letter for you, Lady Isabella," he said, placing it before her.

Puzzled, Isabella picked it up, immediately recognising Silas's handwriting on the front script, which simply bore her name. She looked at him in bewilderment. "Open it," he said gently.

Feeling all eyes on her, she broke the seal on the letter and unfolded the sheet. Quickly, she read:

Dearest Bella,

As I write this letter, I am reminded of Captain Wentworth in Jane Austen's Persuasion. Like him, I am half agony, half hope, for it is time for me to put all my cards on the table and tell you how I feel, and then to ask you a very important question, the answer to which will either make me the happiest or the most miserable of men. I think you must have an inkling as to what it is I wish to ask. It is that thing to do with a ring.

I had wished a private moment to do this in, but your brother has refused to release you from the promise you made, and thus I am compelled to declare myself in the presence of others. *A sign from you will be enough to decide whether I speak those words today or never. I am about to ask whether you would like a slice of pork pie. If your answer is yes, I shall begin my speech. If it is no, I will remain silent. The choice is yours, my darling.*

Yours always,

Silas

Isabella put the letter down with hands that shook and raised her eyes to him. With the gentlest of smiles, he posed the question: "Would you like a slice of pork pie, Bella?"

She took a deep breath and cleared her throat. "Yes, please," she said, quite distinctly.

They exchanged a long, heated look. Then it was Silas's turn to clear his throat. "Bella, I wish to say something to you," he said in a clear voice that reached everyone seated at the picnic. "Our first meeting was not propitious. You turned your nose up at me, and I was boorishly rude. But that day, you took the first piece of my heart. When you bravely saved Samuel, jumping into an icy stream he had fallen into, I lost the next piece of my heart to you. I kissed you that day and gave you more of my poor, beleaguered heart. And then my fate was sealed when I saw you toil tirelessly in the fields, trying to help save the harvest at the Shaw farm. I know that I am far older than you. I do not possess a charming manner and as I have told you many a time, I am no gentleman. But I love you dearly, and if you will do me the great honour of becoming my wife, I will cherish you for the rest of my days."

He knelt before her and took out a ring from his pocket, holding it out to her. "Bella, will you be my wife?"

She wanted to speak, but she could not. Her chest felt so tight, it was nearly impossible to breathe, but her eyes told him everything in her heart, and he smiled.

"Well, what are you waiting for, girl?" said Esther irritably. "Give him an answer."

Immediately, Daniel rose to her defence, saying hotly, "She can take all the time she needs to think about it. We will not rush her."

Still, Isabella could not speak. In desperation, she clutched Silas's hand, the one holding the ring. As ever, he understood. He took her hand and gently slid the ring on her finger. Then he lifted it to his lips for a kiss.

"I think that is a yes," said Theodora.

"I think you may be right," concurred Mrs Corbett.

Isabella's face was now buried in the crook of Silas's neck as he held her tight to him.

"No doubt about it," declared Dr Driscoll. "Now, let us get out the champagne."

Ignoring the voices all around them, Isabella put her lips to Silas's ear and whispered one word. "Yes."

Epilogue

Silas

September 1865, two years later

The carriage rattled noisily along the dusty road on its way towards Netherwick Hall. Inside the vehicle, Silas sat impatiently, eager to arrive home after three days' absence on business in London, which he had spent in protracted meetings with various investors and bankers.

Although Silas had sold off most of his shares in the factories he had set up all those years ago in Manchester, he still took an interest in new manufacturing and engineering ventures as well as in capital markets, making investments wherever he saw fit. In the years since his marriage to Bella, he had continued to increase his fortune substantially through an astute portfolio of such investments. It had kept him usefully occupied, for he had never felt quite comfortable in being simply a country gentleman of leisure.

He tried not to absent himself from home too often, but when he did, as on this latest trip, he was always anxious to return as quickly as possible. When his train had steamed into Oxford station earlier this afternoon, he had been one of the first passengers out, travel case in hand, making his hurried way towards the row of waiting carriages outside. And now, glancing out of the window, he could see ahead the turning that would take them to the main entrance of Netherwick Hall.

No sooner had the carriage stopped than he jumped out and flew up the steps, pressing on the doorbell eagerly. The door was opened by the butler, who ushered him inside and took his case from him. "Good day, Fletcher," he greeted. "All well in my absence?"

"Yes sir, and good day," replied the butler.

"Where can I find my wife, Fletcher?"

"I believe, sir, that Lady Isabella is in her private parlour," replied the butler.

"Thank you, Fletcher," said Silas, already making his way across the hall towards the room on the east side of the house that had been assigned as Bella's private parlour. This was where she sat to do her correspondence, go through the estate accounts or simply to have a quiet space to read a book. He knocked on the door and entered, finding Bella seated at her desk, studying a large leather ledger. She looked up on hearing him enter and beamed. "You are back!" she cried, getting to her feet quickly and running towards him.

Silas shut the door behind him and turned the key in the lock before drawing Bella into his embrace. As their lips came together for a needy kiss, he inhaled the familiar fragrance of orange blossoms. Finally, he felt like he was home. He tightened his grip on her and slipped his tongue into the velvet softness of her mouth, sighing with pleasure. "I've missed you," he growled.

"And I you," she murmured against his lips.

He kissed her some more, grinding his groin to hers and letting her feel the hard length of his aching cock. With a wrench, he pulled himself away and went quickly to the window to draw the curtains. Having ensured their privacy, he faced his wife. "Come here, Bella," he commanded.

She came to him at once, her chest rising up and down with shallow breaths, her eyes dilated. He studied her flushed face a moment, then issued his next instruction. "Take out my cock, Bella, and lick it. I want it nice and wet so I can fuck you."

She dropped to her knees and began to unbutton the fastenings of his trousers. Soon, she had his cock out, her small hands wrapped around its girth. Her tongue came out to lick him in short little laps, like a dainty cat. He groaned and ran his fingers through her hair. "Take me into your mouth," he urged. She widened her lips and took him in as far as she could. The sight of her lips wrapped around his length was one that he never grew tired of. She was magnificent, he thought with feral pride, and she was his. "Go on, darling," he grunted. "Get me nice and wet."

She sucked on his length, alternating with licks, getting him ready as instructed. After a time, he gently withdrew from her mouth and helped her back to her feet. Guiding her towards the desk, he said throatily, "Lean your elbows on here, my love."

Once she was in position, he lifted the skirt of her dress and found the opening of her drawers, pulling the fabric apart to reveal her flesh. A moment later, he had notched his cock to her entrance. "I need to be inside you, my love," he rasped, his mouth nuzzling the back of her neck. "Are you going to take me?"

"Yes, Silas. I need you."

That was all the invitation he required. In one powerful thrust, he drove deep into her. They moaned in unison at the wonderful sensation of being joined, flesh to flesh. He pulled away and thrust again, then again, building a drumming rhythm as he drove into her over and over. He was close to his release, but he had to hold off until she found hers. His hand searched through the layers of petticoats and fabric until he found the slit of her drawers, and then his fingers were on her pleasure nub, stroking her as he continued the savage thrusts of his cock. "Go on, Bella," he growled. "Let it happen."

He gave another hard thrust, close to his own precipice. "Bella!" he roared. And her body obediently pulsed around him as she found her climax. Then in relief, he drove into her once more and released his seed.

He stilled inside her and dropped his forehead to the back of her neck in exhaustion. "Silas," she murmured. "That was... I needed that."

"And me." He slid out of her carefully, and taking out a handkerchief from his pocket, tried to clean her up the best he could before dropping her skirt back into place. Quickly, he tucked himself back into his trousers and tidied himself up, then went to the window and drew back the curtains again.

Now that the most pressing physical need had been sated, they could talk and catch up on all that had happened in his absence. He led her to the settee and sat down beside her, drawing her head to his shoulder. "Tell me all," he said simply. And she recounted the various happenings, from her latest encounter with Farmer Flint, to the harvesting on the Shaw farm, to Samuel falling over and scraping his knee, to Theodora making a beautiful drawing of baby Eliza, and to Eliza, their seven month old daughter, having the beginnings of her first tooth.

Once she had finished, she rested against him in companiable silence, only breaking it once to murmur, "I love you, Silas."

"And I love you."

He supposed he should bestir himself to go check on the rest of his household, but he was too comfortable for the moment to move an inch. Their haven of contentment was to be interrupted a moment later, however, by a sharp knock on the door. Remembering that he had it locked, Silas got to his feet and went to open it. A footman stood outside, a note in his hand. "This just arrived from Stanton Hall, sir."

"Thank you," Silas said, taking the note and shutting the door again. Glancing down, he saw it was addressed to Bella in her brother Daniel's writing. He handed it to her and watched as she broke the seal and read.

"Oh!" she cried.

"What is it?" he asked sharply. In answer, she gave him the note. He read it quickly.

Dear Bella,

Good news! A telegram just came in from Papa to say Benjamin is home safe and sound from the war. He wants us all to visit home as soon as we can. Are you up for a trip to Ohio? I'll be going to London tomorrow to book a passage on the first ship possible. Let me know by return if you're up for it, and I'll book us all on the ship.

Yours,

Daniel

"Benjamin is home safe!" she exclaimed. Next moment, she burst into tears—happy tears, Silas presumed.

He pulled her into his arms and soothed her the best he could. "Benjamin is safe," he repeated. "And now I can finally get to meet my other brother-in-law and your parents too."

"Are you all right to go straight away?" she asked between her tears.

"I shall have to make some arrangements for my absence, but it can be done. And besides, there may be a few business prospects I can look into while we are in America." He kissed the top of her head and added, "The children will be excited when we tell them."

"Yes," she murmured, then drew back. "Come on, Silas. Let's go find them."

He stayed her a moment, putting both hands to her face and looking into her eyes. "Happy, Bella?" he asked.

"Very happy," she smiled.

He kissed her lips gently. "Then let's go share the good news," he said, taking hold of her hand.

Afterword

Dear reader,

I hoped you enjoyed this spin-off novella from **The Stanton Legacy** series. You may also be interested to read another novella linked to this series, **Mr Templeton Finds Himself a Wife**.

Please also consider subscribing to my newsletter on **mmwakeford.substack.com** to get latest authorly news, book recommendations and freebies.

May I ask you for a small favour?

Reviews are the life blood of independent authors. Please could you help spread the word about this book by submitting a review on **Amazon**, **Goodreads** or any other book reader platform. Thank you!

M.M. Wakeford

About the author

M.M. Wakeford lives with her husband and son in a London terraced house that gathers dust while she loses herself in her writing. A lifelong reader of romantic novels, she writes in many genres including contemporary, sci-fi and historical romance. All her stories strive to capture that heady feeling of falling in love, with authentic characters whose journey to a happily ever after is lined with dilemmas to overcome. If you're looking for a page turning romance with high emotion and a good dose of spice, you've come to the right place.

Also by this author

THE VISCOUNT'S SCANDALOUS AFFAIR
Book 1 – The Stanton Legacy

"Why not have a short dalliance with me? In the cold desert of my spinsterhood, I assure you I will not treasure my virtue half as much as the memories of sensual pleasures with you."

Life has not been kind to Charlotte Harding. Orphaned, impoverished and plain-looking, she depends on the charity of relatives who take her in when she has nowhere else to go. In their London home, she meets the rich and handsome Viscount Stanton who is promised to the beautiful heiress, Miss Powell. Charlotte is smitten with him on first sight, but the Viscount barely notices her except to note her unprepossessing looks and shabby dress.

One night at a society ball, Charlotte accidentally witnesses a secret tryst between the viscount and his mistress - and is unfortunately discovered. Her silence is bought with an unforgettable kiss that leaves Charlotte yearning for more. So when she learns that the viscount has ended his relationship with his mistress, Charlotte seizes the opportunity to make him a scandalous offer - a short, discreet affair in return for memories to treasure in her spinsterhood.

Author's note: The Viscount's Scandalous Affair is a historical romance written in a homage to Jane Austen and Georgette

Heyer, with a dose of spice. It features an illicit affair between two unlikely lovers whose emotional and bumpy journey into love ends in a happily ever after.

What people say about The Viscount's Scandalous Affair

"A beautiful story… and the ending was perfection." **Goodreads review**

"Excellent book to curl up with and enjoy. What a way to start a new series. Would strongly recommend." **Goodreads review**

"A stunning read and a great story… compelling and very steamy." **Goodreads review**

"Love this book! Please add this to your TBR lists. This book was explosive from the first chapter and left me wanting more. Great book and a great choice." **Goodreads review**

"An amazing regency romance where you'll feel all the emotions. A mix of twists, forgiveness, angst, steam, drama, love and a second chance at life. So beautifully written." **Di – Amazon review**

"It's hard not to fall in love with Charlotte… This was a charming book and I loved every second of it." **Ashleigh – Goodreads review**

"This book has it all… hold on to your pantalettes! Very raw and scandalous. There is a happy ever after so dive in with your heart open and you won't be disappointed!" **Janine – Amazon review**

MELINDA'S CHOICE

Two very different men, and yet I want them both. I can't have my cake and eat it though. I have to make a choice.

Melinda Garcia, recently appointed Earth Federation's ambassador to the planet Krovatia, is a career woman going places... and leaving behind a broken marriage to the man she still loves.

For the last two decades, there has only been one woman in Wyatt's life. Yet his inability to get on a spaceship and leave Earth has cost him. Is there any way to win Melinda back?

Kirimor, a powerful male with five lovely drashas—concubines that service his needs as the most senior priest of Krovatia—has fallen for the lovely Earth female, but will she accept him as he is?

Two different men who love her. One difficult choice to make.

Author's note: Melinda's Choice is a steamy science-fiction romance featuring a love triangle between a strong, determined woman, the man she loves and the sexy alien with a tail that sweeps her off her feet.

What people say about Melinda's Choice:

"This book was so good! I binged it in a day I couldn't put it down! ...THE SPICE was so so so hot!? If you want a sci-fi. Hot aliens, love triangle! Heartbreak, healing, betrayal, angst, it had it all and I loved it all." **Amazon review**

"A great alien romance/ fated mates... This book will have you feeling all the emotions as you journey with Melinda throughout the story...I definitely recommend this book for my fellow alien romance lovers!" **Amazon review**

"Sexy aliens with tails, with a heartbreaking twist and then a HEA? If you like sci-fi, romance and smut I think you're going to love this book! I enjoyed how the love triangle was set up in a way that you had a hard time deciding who Melinda should choose! ...This book was really fun to read! Total page turner and the spice 🌶" **Goodreads review**

"O.M.F.G! This was my first sci-fi romance and let me tell you... I'm forever obsessed! ... I never in a million years would ever think I'd be into alien smut... and tail play... but damn... that's all I gotta say." **Amazon review**

"This has become one of my favorite all-time sci-fi novels. It has a hero and heroine who are older, so we get to see many fascinating dynamics in their relationship. We also get to see how they honor each other's cultures and are willing to learn about them. Melinda's Choice has many reasons for me to love it." **Amazon review**

Milton Keynes UK
Ingram Content Group UK Ltd.
UKHW020654150824
446997UK00010B/245